TWO ACTION-PACKED WESTERNS FOR ONE LOW PRICE!

RIMROCK VENGEANCE

Curt's eyes turned to the man sitting with legs outstretched before him. Keogh crossed and examined the man curiously. At his sharply indrawn breath, Curt bounced to his feet.

"What's wrong?" he asked.

"Looks like plenty," Keogh returned, his voice suddenly grim. "I used to know this man."

"He's been here for quite a spell—judging by his appearances."

"Quite a while," Keogh agreed. He indicated a small hole in the back of the man's coat. Such a hole could only have been made by a bullet. "Shot in the back."

THE SHERIFF OF SINGING RIVER

Levinger's Colt was out and spitting lead as Boone cleared the last several feet in a sudden leap. At most times in the past, even the day before, in a similar situation, he'd have gone for his own gun, trying to reach it first. The odds had shifted when he'd accepted the star glittering on his shirt.

A move for his gun would mean that Moon Star would back Levinger with their guns. For them there were only blacks and whites, with no grays. War was war and you fought—to the death—to win.

Other *Leisure Books* by Al Cody:
RIM OF THE RANGE/THUNDER TO THE WEST

RIMROCK VENGEANCE/ THE SHERIFF OF SINGING RIVER

AL CODY

LEISURE BOOKS   NEW YORK CITY

A LEISURE BOOK®

August 1993

Published by

Dorchester Publishing Co., Inc.
276 Fifth Avenue
New York, NY 10001

RIMROCK VENGEANCE Copyright © MCMLXV by Al Cody
THE SHERIFF OF SINGING RIVER Copyright © MCMLXV
by Al Cody

Printed in the United States of America.

RIMROCK VENGEANCE

1.

The bullet came out of nowhere, buzzing like an angry wasp. It tore past Keogh's left ear with a vicious whine, eclipsed a moment later by the thunderous blast of the gun which had sent it on its way. Had there been any room for doubt as to the weapon, that booming roar dispelled it. The shot had come from a rifle, and when the odds both of distance and a moving target were considered, whoever had squeezed the trigger had to be counted a marksman.

Keogh jerked instinctively, half-turning in the saddle, his normally bland profile sharpened. The movement saved his life. A second slug of lead made itself heard, but this one came from nearly the opposite direction, as the echoing boom of the gun indicated. It had been intended to hit between the eyes instead of in the back.

A third bullet, following hard, was better aimed, or worse, according to the point of view. It also missed Keogh, but it struck his horse. It sounded like a hammer hard-driven against the flesh, and the cayuse staggered blindly. Keogh managed to kick free, landing in a rolling dive in the grass and narrowly escaping being pinned down by the collapsing horse.

The grass grew short and stubby. Cured by the summer sun, it was needle-like under wrists and hands. Keogh twisted and crawled, jerking loose his own revolver as he took shelter behind the dead horse. His hat had fallen off, revealing hair of a sandy hue, matching his complexion. The light blue eyes seemed to view the world with a mild surprise.

One hind hoof of the fallen horse, painfully drawn up in its final agony, kicked back sharply in a final throe, narrowing missing his head. It raked the ground, stirring a puff of dust.

Sprawling flat, Keogh reached absently for his hat with his free hand, eyes raking the landscape in an intent survey. That the murderous attack was not directed solely against himself was already apparent. Curt, whose horse had been ambling sleepily about a length behind his own, was also having difficulties. With Keogh down if not out, Curt was now the target for the assassins' bullets. Both heavy guns continued to boom from opposite directions, and one of the ambushers loped into sight, firing as he came. A clump of distant cottonwoods had provided cover while he waited.

He came at a gallop, and the sun lanced like flame along the rifle barrel. Made over-confident by Keogh's fall, the fellow was closing in for the kill.

So sweeping a run might not be as brash as it looked. Curt had been lucky enough to escape the first murderous fusillade, and his horse had also gone unhit; but the buzzing death whining about its ears had spooked the cayuse. It was attempting to take the bit in its teeth and head for other parts, and Curt was making an equally determined effort to halt it where it was, while he discovered what had happened to his partner. Frantic, the cayuse bucked wildly, and Curt made an equally impromptu descent. He hit the ground all spraddled out; then the cayuse was desperately plunging away.

Had any doubt remained as to the murderous intentions of the bushwhack pair, they were removed as the oncoming rider slowed to a walk, and the lance took on the semblance of a rifle, leveled for the kill, snout swinging where Curt sprawled, momentarily dazed. The whiplash sound of Keogh's gun blended with the heavier cough of the rifle.

The range was long for a forty-five, but his shot accomplished as much as he hoped for, disconcerting the rifleman's aim. At the return of the compliment he pulled up suddenly, then veered away, and Curt came scrambling, gopher-like, on hands and knees. His hat, too, had fallen off, revealing black hair now which was overlong, but not incongruous with the silky mustache.

"Whew!" he gasped, taking up a position beside Keogh. "You figure maybe we were expected?"

"This don't exactly have the earmarks of a welcoming party," Keogh conceded, and sought to make himself smaller as he took stock of the situation. Curt's cayuse, finding itself no longer a target, was coming to a stop, but hopelessly beyond reach. Keogh's horse was dead. That left them not merely afoot, but trapped between a pair of determined killers.

Both gunmen had put in an appearance now, coming, like their first shots, from opposite directions. They had been at opposite sides of the course which Keogh and Curt had been following, taking advantage of twin patches of cover. Each was about a quarter of a mile away from the victims, with no shelter between. Only the body of the horse afforded a measure of protection against rifle bullets.

The trouble with such a fort was that, while it afforded cover from one direction, the other gunman had an unobstructed view, and both men were exposed, each to one enemy. Equipped with rifles, which outranged six-guns, the bushwhackers could pick off their victims while safe from reprisal.

"I'm beginnin' to get the impression that maybe we ain't wanted hereabouts," Curt observed. "Either these folks have a suspicious nature, or else they ain't inclined to take chances."

"I'll go along with that on both counts," Keogh agreed. The two gunmen had halted, each staring at the dead horse and the forted-up pair beside it, then looking questioningly at each other. One waved an arm in a signal which his companion seemed to understand. They made no attempt to join forces, preferring to come at their victims from two sides. They were making one concession to an uncertain target and the guns which might menace them by dismounting. Leaving their horses to stand ground-hitched, they started to wriggle forward down on hands and knees.

That way, they could come within sure range, while remaining safe from the short guns. There was no place to retreat before so murderous a threat; at least not much of a place.

That seemed to add irony to the situation. There was a break almost at hand, but hardly a promising one. The one gunman had been ahead and to the north; the second man, who had opened the firing, behind and to the east.

Curt, who had been heading toward a line of rimrocks, had almost reached the ridge as the shooting commenced. No more than a dozen or so feet to the side, though scarcely visible as they lay there, a rocky cliff dropped away sheerly to lower ground. Keogh had been able to obtain a fairly good look before the interruption.

By a sudden fast move, either or both of them might be able to scramble the dozen or so feet and duck over the brink, putting themselves temporarily out of sight of the gunmen. They might be potted while making the attempt, but taking the chance was preferable to waiting to be shot like sitting ducks.

The difficulty was that Keogh had observed a straight drop below the rimrocks of at least a hundred feet, in some places twice that, to the grassy stretches where the land again leveled off. Stepping off into such space would break a man's neck.

Still, the rimrocks offered shelter, if it could be used. Keogh's lariat was within hand reach, tied alongside the saddle-horn. He eyed it speculatively, regretfully. One end would have to remain anchored to the saddle-horn. If he went over the rim and down, rope's end would still find him at least eighty-five feet in space; probably more.

He would be like a spider dangling on its web, but with one fatal difference. A spider could lengthen its strand according to the need. There was no way of lengthening the rope so as to reach the base of the rimrocks safely.

Not that there would be any assurance of safety even at the foot of the cliff. Once the riflemen reached the crest, they could still pick their targets off at leisure, while they themselves remained out of sight. The possible gain was there might be some small hole in the cliff where they could fort up and at least make a fight of it.

The killers were taking their time, making a slow but safe approach, withholding their fire until they could be certain of their targets. That would not be long.

"Those fellers sure don't aim to take any chances —or to give us any," Curt sighed, and fingered his revolver regretfully. He had recovered from a momentary daze, though a long rip in his right shirt sleeve testified to the force with which he had been thrown. The exposed flesh was bruised and bloody.

Keogh nodded in sober agreement. It was an accurate assessment, unless they could find some method to counter the methodical way in which that pair were going about the business of murder. Not being novices at that sort of game, both had anticipated the possibility of trouble, but neither had envisioned an attack which might kill them in cold blood before they were even near their objective. Clearly, someone was willing to go to any lengths to cover up crimes already committed and to maintain a system which from all reports was proving rather profitable.

The pair of gunmen were old hands at the game, as their moves demonstrated. Against novices, there might be a chance for counter-action, but these killers wouldn't expose themselves.

Keogh's glance returned to the lariat. Speculatively he studied the crest of the rimrock, then glanced on to where the gunman who had first fired was crawling. He was almost within revolver range, but like them, virtually invisible in the cover of grass. He was also somewhat lower down, since to the east the land dropped away in a gradual slope.

Keogh jerked at the saddle-strap, loosening the knot

which held the coil of rope. It would be a long chance, but there might be a possibility. However long the odds, it was better to buck them than to wait for the inevitable.

The coiled lariat was partly held down by the weight of the horse. Keogh tugged it free, tying one end to the saddle-horn. The noose at the opposite end he closed over his right foot.

Curt was watching, his face indicating his puzzlement. He, too, had had a look over the side as they rode.

"It's a long way down," he observed.

Keogh nodded. "A far distance," he agreed, "like the trail we've followed together, Curt. Maybe there's a chance."

Curt shook his head, not understanding. "You'd break every bone in your body."

"What would be the difference as coyote bait?" Keogh's smile was tight. He was ten years older than Curt, thirty pounds lighter as well as three inches shorter. But he was as wiry as whipcord, and as strong as his handsome side-kick. That part of the task shouldn't be too demanding.

"I figure that if I make it over the rim, that will take them by surprise," he confided. "And from a few feet down, the angle may be right so that I can get a better view of our visitor. At least there's a chance."

Curt nodded hopefully. It did offer a possibility. Dangling over the side, holding to the rope with one hand, the loop about his foot, then working his Colt's with his other hand, just might work. The angle of the slope, with a dip in the rimrock behind, might expose the crawling gunman. The rifleman might shoot back, and that would be a fantastic duel, with Keogh clinging like a spider on its web. But he might be able to force the issue.

Much would depend on surprise. Should he choose to wait, shrinking low in the grass, the gunman would hold all the trumps. But, finding himself suddenly under fire from a new angle, he might not consider all the angles. Keogh was taking the risk that he'd fight back. The dead horse would then be a real shelter for Curt, the odds reduced by half.

2.

Keogh moved fast, scuttling for the edge of the rim-rock like a gopher before the swoop of a hawk. He reached the brink before the surprised gunman could properly aim, and the crash of the rifle was the only indication that he'd tried. Keogh went over the side.

He descended fast enough so that the hemp was rough and hot against his palms, but the loop about his foot checked the slide, leaving him spinning in space. Considerably farther below than it had seemed in that initial survey from the saddle, the ground sloped away again. A surprised bird darted out from a nest on the cliff-side, well under him.

Clinging with his left hand, he jerked his revolver with the other. The sudden gyrating was a problem he had not foreseen, and he was hindered as the rope twisted, facing the cliff-side, then outward, before the vista he wanted came into view. Action had to be fast, which mitigated against accuracy, and only luck of his own surprise movement gave him a chance. The rifleman, after getting off that quick shot, had come up to his knees, excited and apprehensive about something he hadn't expected and did not yet quite understand.

Keogh fired, and apparently the bullet was close. The gunman cringed; then he understood the ruse and came on the run, confident that attack was the best defense.

Keogh was hardly in a position to argue that. The still twisting rope turned him away at a moment, dangling, an inviting target, unable his enemy. The rifleman was shooting as he ran, demonstrating familiarity with the long gun and also excitement. One bullet struck the rock wall at shoulder height and caromed off with a pinging whistle, scattering flecks of stone. A second nudged the rope, jerking like a blow, a savage finger on a fiddle-string.

The nudge proved helpful, turning the rope more quickly, bringing his opponent back into view. In the interval he'd covered a hundred feet, and now was within six-gun range. He halted in sudden realization, swinging the stock of the rifle to his shoulder, sighting to make sure. Keogh was a short distance ahead.

He heard the smash of the heavier lead against the cliff behind, felt the sharp spatter of loosened flakes, but now he could holster his gun and climb. While doing so, he became aware of other guns keeping up the chant, one distant and savage. A closer sound was that of the six-gun in Curt's hand.

Both ceased, leaving a sudden heavy silence as he

reached the crest and strove to pull himself over it. Then Curt's hands were grasping his own, tugging him the last few feet, and he could collapse suddenly on solid ground and allow the earth to heave as it would, while he fought a tendency to be sick.

That passed, and he got to his feet and looked about. Curt was punching empty shells from his gun, making a chore of reloading, his face showing strain.

"All over, Keogh," he observed soberly. "My man excited and jumped to his feet, too, and that was what I'd been waiting for. You sure outthought them on that deal."

Examination confirmed what they had expected: that both gunmen were dead. It had been a desperate duel at the last, of lever-action rifles against six-guns, but excitement and sudden desperation had betrayed the gunmen into dangerous exposure.

One man had a long, horse-like face, its bony outlines even harsher in death. The other man Keogh guessed to be half-Indian. Both were strangers to them. There was nothing in their pockets to give any clue as to who might have sent them on the bushwhack mission.

One horse afforded a possible clue, bearing the brand OX on its left hip. The other horse was unbranded. Keogh looked thoughtfully from it to his own animal.

"Might be our luck's taking one good turn," he observed. "What do you think, Curt?"

Understanding, Curt studied both horses carefully, nodding in agreement.

"They're both bays, and this one's close to being a dead ringer—or maybe a live one—for your horse," he conceded. "Put your saddle on him, and it'll take a sharp-eyed man, someone who knew this horse to start with, to tell the difference."

"We might find such a person, but since I'm afoot, it's worth chancing." Keogh nodded. "And since his rider killed my horse, it seems a fair enough trade. We'll leave the other horse run free. Somebody would be sure to recognize it."

"What about them?" Curt asked, and gestured. "The ground's hard for digging, even if we had a shovel."

"We'll have to manage it; otherwise questions will be asked—it will be as well if there are not too many answers to be found. Besides, I guess we owe them a burial. There's no assurance that anybody else would give them one."

It required nearly a mile of circling to find a way down from the rimrock, and still more searching along the base of the cliff to locate a place suited to their needs. High water had gashed a ditch during some flash flood. There was a section of overhang, which was not too hard to cave above the bodies. They concealed the operation with a scattering of old brush from a clump which grew nearby.

"Do we take the rifles?" Curt asked. "Spoils of

war? Besides, they have a handy reach."

Keogh considered, then shook his head regretfully.

"We've done pretty well with what we have," he decided. "Being as broke as we are, they could be sold—but they'd likely be recognized by someone, and they'd be out to revenge these fellows. If a dead horse is found, it won't have too much meaning. Someone will likely get curious when this party don't show up or report back, but this is a wide country. It's a long chance anything else will be found this far from the horse, and that should give us some leeway. So I guess we'd better just be on our way, as though nothing had happened."

Curt nodded. Keogh was in charge, and he had a lot of respect for Keogh's judgment.

"You think we can steal in and take anybody by surprise now?"

"Nothing like trying," Keogh said cheerfully. "After sending out such a reception committee, they probably won't be expecting us, at least not till those two fail to report back. Still, this calls for a change of strategy. Either they knew we were coming, or took a chance that strangers might be nosy. I was going as Andrew K. Davidson, you as Ralph C. Lindley— which are good names. But I'll think of something else—if given a chance. Maybe you'd better be Curt Conners."

"You think somebody might have recognized you along the way?"

Keogh considered, then shook his head.

"It's a possibility, but not likely. It's half a dozen years since I was through this part of the country. I've seen no one that looked familiar, and it's not likely that anyone who knew me is still around. I incline to the notion that nosy strangers—any strangers—aren't wanted right now. You'll have to sacrifice those whiskers, I'm afraid. I know they're your pride and joy, but they would be remembered—in case."

Curt sighed, but worked dutifully as a small fire was kindled and water heated. "Wish we had something to cook over that blaze," he observed wistfully. "I'm getting mighty sharp-set."

"Too bad we're broke and out of grub," Keogh returned. "We'll take the bull by the horns and turn in at the XT when we reach it—which should be in time for supper. Maybe we'll get a job there as hands."

Smooth-cheeked now, Curt nodded, feeling a thrill of excitement. The XT, if reports were correct, was at the heart of the conspiracy they were commissioned to resolve. After that murderous attempt on their lives, no doubt remained that they were getting into something big and hardly to be described as pleasant.

There was no question in his mind, either, of turning back. Not only was there a job to do, but this had suddenly become a personal matter. That pair of gunman had been hirelings, sent to stop them, but the man or men who had set a price on their heads would still be waiting.

"Rustling," Curt murmured. "It must really be a big deal, for sure."

"I'm wondering," Keogh confessed. "Ordinarily rustling adds up to a lynch party, and that's the end of it. This time, the boot's been on the other foot—so far."

Keogh whistled plaintively between his teeth as they continued on toward the hills, a jumble of wild country which marked the transition between plain and mountain, and betokened journey's end—a term suddenly fraught with double meaning.

They had followed a devious trail in coming this far, giving every outward appearance of being two footloose cowboys in search of a hard-to-find job. Had the ruse failed somewhere along the way and their disguise been penetrated, or had the attempt to bushwhack them been merely a form of insurance, employed against any suspicious stranger?

The rub was that whether the answer was negative or positive seemed to make remarkably little difference.

Word of the job which was to be done had reached them at Broken Bow, and they had set out, swinging up through the Nebraska country with the last of the winter snows spitting like squalling cats in their faces. It would have been possible to take the new iron horse, since the railroad was all but completed as far as their destination, at a big saving of time. But Keogh had figured that this sort of an arrival might enable them to pick up a few clues, and would probably be less apt to excite suspicion.

The sudden downpours of spring had drenched them while the Dakotas turned green with promise. Now the summer sun baked the Montana prairie, and their long-suffering cayuses began to grow footsore and hoof-worn.

Therein lay the chief identifiable difference between Keogh's new mount and the animal which lay dead. Both were of a color and size, and neither animal had ever known the sting of a branding iron. But eyes as keen as Keogh's might detect the difference between Keogh's mount and Curt's. It was more than unworn hoofs; it was a freshness and vitality unsapped by the miles.

His tune was "The Mississippi Sawyer," a low-keyed, plaintive variation. One well-browned hand held the reins in a mechanical gesture, since his new mount seemed to require no conscious direction. With his other hand, Keogh jingled a collection of coins, two dimes and a two-bit piece. These, as Curt was painfully aware, represented their total cash assets, all that remained of the expense account which had been advanced them.

Temptation had assailed Curt a week before, the urge to sit in on a friendly game of poker. It had turned out to be less friendly than he had anticipated.

His own hand of four queens had been topped by an equal run of kings. Spang in the middle of the game he'd found himself ousted, their cash resources, of which he'd been the custodian, evaporated rather than enhanced.

Keogh had lifted sandy eyebrows in an oblique grin, but had refrained from recriminations. Save for a lack of working capital, they looked like what they were: a pair of cowboys, lean and competent. Men riding the grub line could count on a welcome, a meal and a bunk overnight at any ranch along the way.

The trouble was that across these wide and empty reaches, outfits were few and far apart.

The prairie had been left behind, and the land turned rough, with a thrust of hills ahead. The XT, Curt knew, was a big spread, and this must be a part of it. There were those who whispered, or even had the temerity to voice aloud, their suspicions that much of that bigness was the outgrowth of rustling.

The loss or stealing of cattle was not unusual on any range; cattlemen took it almost as a matter of course. An occasional necktie party generally kept such stealing within reasonable bounds.

But here the situation seemed to be out of control. Not only scattered animals but whole herds had a way of vanishing. The culminating outrage had been the sale to the army post commanded by Major Yancey Tombright of a thousand head branded XT.

Duly delivered to the post, they had been as promptly spirited away from under the noses of the garrison. Every effort to trail or recover them had failed.

The major had taken that as a personal affront, with the result that Keogh had been sent for.

Suspicion might point strongly in one or two directions, but suspicion was not proof, nor did it put meat on a platter. Clearly, others who might also be interested had heard that men of ability had been sent for.

Now they were on the XT, and here at last were scattered cattle, peacefully grazing. The herd was fat and sleek.

In the distance loomed the ranch buildings, and everywhere was a look of prosperity. But something was amiss.

"This is the XT?" Curt demanded.

"Supposed to be," Keogh admitted. But something was wrong. These cattle wore a different brand, a Double Diamond I.

3.

Both men studied the cattle as they rode through the scattered herd. Outwardly there was nothing wrong with the brand which adorned their left hips. But their were none with the XT, and there was a disturbing similarity. The XT was also supposed to be on the left hip.

It was unnecessary, thanks to the understanding between them, to mention that an XT might have been altered and enlarged with a running iron to form the new brand. Given enough time, the fresh burn would heal and a new crop of hair grow out, leaving everything with a normal appearance.

It was within the bounds of possibility that something like that could have happened here. The sale to the Army had taken place the previous fall. There had been time enough. But why would anyone flaunt such a herd almost under the noses of the Army garrison and Major Yancey Tombright? Should these cattle, by some coincidence, be the stolen herd, why had they not been sold and butchered?

"It don't exactly make sense," Curt muttered, and Keogh nodded, understanding his thought processes. It didn't make sense. But then, a great deal about this case had baffled those who had tried to solve it.

"Who owns this outfit?" Curt asked. The cattle hardly raised their heads as they picked a way among them. Men on horses were no novelty.

"A man named Desmond, from what I've been told," Keogh returned. "Carl Desmond."

"I've got a feeling we're riding into something," Curt muttered. He rubbed his stomach thoughtfully. "Let's hope they feed us before they start shooting."

From the buildings ahead, twin columns of smoke arose like welcoming beacons. One drifted from the cook shack pipe; the other curled from the stone chimney of a sprawling log house. Curtains fluttered from open windows in a tempering breeze. Such a sight was surprising, but was explained as a woman appeared in the doorway, peering out at them. Her interest seemed frank and unembarrassed, and Curt's amazement grew as he saw that she was young. The afternoon sun seemed to tangle in her hair, turning it to a bright halo.

A second woman looked briefly over her shoulder before turning back. The sun's gleam was in Curt's eyes.

"Did you see what I saw, Keogh?" His whisper was hoarse, not quite believing. "There's more'n cattle been transplanted here—an angel 'stead of just a woman!"

The girl caught his glance, if not his words, and appeared to be confused. Color flowed in her cheeks. She turned back also, somewhat hastily.

Keogh was not much surprised by his companion's reaction. Curt was always susceptible to the sight of a pretty girl. But this time he was more stirred than usual. That might be accounted for by the fact that women, of any age or degree of good looks, had been rare along the trail they had followed.

"XT or Double Diamond or rainbow's end, it looks like we've landed right in the middle of paradise," Curt went on. "Glory be! If I'm dreamin', don't wake me up!"

It had happened fast, but Curt was clearly smitten, and deeply. Keogh made an abrupt decision, but his face gave no outward indication of it. Other men were appearing, clustering near the doors of the bunkhouse or the adjoining cook shack. Apparently the crew had just come in from the range and were awaiting the call to supper.

Curt's nose cleaved the air, testing like a fox hound's. Twin fragrances were wafted on the afternoon breeze. These were unmistakably the blends of cookery from the two kitchens meeting and mingling, each savory enough to be sorted out by a knowing nose.

Keogh guessed that the main course for the crew would be stew, probably with hot biscuits, a mouth-watering combination for a hungry man. At the big house, where the owner lived with his wife and daughter, the aroma was unquestionably of chicken, topped by dumplings. It had been a long time, a very long while indeed, since he had tasted stewed chicken and dumplings, but its subtle fragrance was unforgettable. Also, if his nose was not deceived, there was the hint of fresh, apple pie, just taken hot from the oven. Curt's designation of paradise might not be too wide of the mark.

On the other hand, this had been the XT, enough in itself to cause most travelers to swing wide around the big ranch. Most of the lounging crew made no move, but they were watching with more sharpness than a pair of wandering cowpokes normally merited, stiffening, with menace and hostility on every face.

Curt's mind was momentarily bemused. His horse had been swinging instinctively toward the group clustered near the bunkhouse and the barn beyond. He was startled as Keogh headed straight toward the big house instead. Even for a man full of gall and vinegar, such a course was brazen, and in this case it was doubly so. But Curt followed his lead as a matter of course.

Two men had been giving particular attention to their approach. One, standing near the bunkhouse, appeared of two minds as to what course to follow. He looked toward the other man, who, hands on hips, gave a slight nod. Detaching himself from the crew, the owner sauntered across to the now empty doorway, where the women had appeared a few moments earlier. He planted himself there as if on guard.

Keogh was forced to make a swift decision, an equally abrupt change of plans. There was no sign of recognition on the face of the boss, but that would follow swiftly and inevitably, and had better be met head on. Suspicion was rife in the minds of every man of the crew.

The owner's eyes remained blank, hooded, but his gaze was calculating, faintly challenging. Most cowboys knew of the reputation of this ranch, and gave it a wide berth. Those brash enough to venture in kept their place, and that place was the bunkhouse, not the dwelling where the boss hung his hat.

Keogh gave no indication he sensed a barrier. He swung down from the saddle, dropping the bridle reins and gazing around with open approval. His nod was casual.

"Looks like you've done pretty well for yourself, Hendricks," he observed. "I take it this is your outfit now. I was told we'd find a good bunch of beef here, but I didn't expect quite so nice a lot."

Hendricks was taken by surprise and showed it. Some of the suspicion faded from his eyes, for he was clearly pleased at the compliment. Curt put him down as an easygoing sort, easily swayed.

"I guess they ain't too bad, considerin'," he granted, and eyed Keogh closely, clearly uncertain.

Only one assumption seemed reasonable. This pair of riders must have been observed and passed as harmless by the reception committee.

"Keogh," he said. "Last time I saw you, you were over a Hardscrabble Creek. You've come a long way from there." He extended a hand, seeing the suspicion and tension gradually dissipate. Apparently it was not known exactly who was being sent into this country, and the pair of gunmen must have acted on general principles.

"This is my partner, Curt Conners." Keogh surprised Curt in turn with his next words.

"We're cattle buyers. Heard there was a good bunch here and rode to have a look."

Curt had his face under control as he too swung down. Why, the gall of him! he reflected admiringly, and thought ruefully of the small change which constituted their total capital. But when he made a bluff, Keogh always made it a good one.

"That so?" Hendricks' manner underwent a subtle change. "Glad to see you again, Keogh. Cattle buyer, eh? You've come up some in the world yourself. Well, a man can't stand still, and I guess we ain't been exactly slidin' back."

Hendricks was secretly relieved. Newcomers were always to be viewed with suspicion, but the fact that these fellows were here was in their favor, and Keogh, as far as he remembered, had been a harmless enough sort. Their arrival would mean a pleasant break in the monotony, especially for his women-folks.

Hendricks was probably as democratic as most cat-tlemen, a man who worked shoulder to shoulder with his crew at whatever job needed doing. Frequently he ate with them, associating with them on terms of equality, but only up to a certain point. He was proud of his own rise in the world, and like most employers, he made a subtle but unmistakable distinction be-tween himself and his hands.

A cowboy, particularly one looking for a job or riding the grub line, would be welcome to a meal or a bed—on this ranch as well as on any other—but that was all, and it was the same with the rest of the crew.

A cattle buyer, however, was something else, oc-cupying a different and distinctly higher rating in the social scale. Many thoughts were clashing and con-flicting in Hendricks' mind, among them one common to all fathers of daughters of marriageable age. He made his decision, pushing possibly troublesome con-flicts into the background.

"Glad to see you again," Hendricks went on, and shook both their hands cordially. "You're just in time for supper. The boys will look after your horses." His voice was not raised, but a pair of the group by the cook house advanced promptly to lead the animals away. Apparently the horse which Keogh rode failed to stir any suspicion. "Come along inside. I expect the women-folks will rustle up something to eat."

He led the way into the house, pausing to introduce his wife, then his daughter, as she appeared at the doorway behind her mother, between the kitchen and the dining room. Both women came forward shyly to shake hands, clearly surprised yet pleased at having company. Curt, bemused, was aware of a soft yet firm hand in his. Miss Elizabeth's eyes were bright as well as friendly. She exclaimed at his torn shirt sleeve and bruised and bloody arm.

"Mercy! How did that happen?"

"Horse jumped at a rabbit—caught me sort of dreamin', and jumped right out from under me," Curt said. "Sort of tore the sleeve, I guess."

"Why, it's all bruised and bloody. You wash up, and then I'll put some salve on it. It might be serious."

"And I'll set a couple of extra places," Mrs. Hendricks added. "It won't take but a minute."

"Now don't go to any fuss on our account," Keogh protested. "Though it will be nice to wash up a bit—"

"There's plenty of soap and water," Hendricks assured them, and led the way to an outside corner, on the shaded side of the house off the kitchen. A nominal number of flies clustered on the screen door, attracted by the odors of cookery, clinging so stickily as to indicate the approach of a storm. There was a pump, a tin wash basin on a wooden bench, and soap. Elizabeth brought them a towel, also a clean shirt.

"Put this on," she instructed Curt. "It's one of

Daddy's. I'll sew up the tear in yours after supper."

"Why, thank you, ma'am—Miss Elizabeth," Curt managed, toweling his face vigorously. "It's most kind of you to take so much trouble. But you shouldn't go to so much bother on my account."

"It's no trouble," she assured him serenely. "I'll be glad to." She returned presently with a salve, and rubbed it on the scratches.

"I'll feel better knowing that it's properly cared for," she said. "And don't call me ma'am or Miss Elizabeth. I wouldn't know who you meant. I'm Betty."

"Betty's always been my favorite name for a woman," Curt assured her. "And I'm Curt." He colored to the roots of his hair at such forwardness, adding hastily, "I'm right obliged."

"Supper's on the table," she returned, and vanished quickly back inside.

Keogh was studying Curt attentively as he used the towel in turn. Curt colored anew, and caught a glimpse of himself in the small mirror fastened at the side of the porch. Around its diamond rim, on all four sides, in bold but fading letters, ran the inscription: "Cactus Valley Hardware. Saddles, Harness, Farm Implements, Hay and Feed. The Best Place to Trade."

With sudden approval, Curt noted the smoothness of his cheeks, shaved only that afternoon, the neatness of the shirt which he now wore, however faded from many launderings. Then he whispered to Keogh as Keogh ran a comb through his hair:

"Dang it, Keogh, we might have found us a job here! Which should be a proper set-up!"

Keogh grinned as he returned the steel comb to its place beside the mirror.

"So we might," he conceded. "But do you think Papa would let his darling daughter look twice at one of the hands—even if she was so inclined?"

Curt lingered a moment before following Keogh inside, to allow the fresh flush to subside from his cheeks. There were times when Keogh was uncannily observant. And, as usual, he was right.

4.

The meal left nothing to be desired, even for hungry men who had been eating irregularly. Not only were there dumplings with the chicken, but they came light as a dream from the kettle, and the gravy had a natural affinity for the mashed potatoes. The pie was not only apple, but, even more surprising, the apples were fresh, the crust flaky. Both women laughingly gave credit to the other for the tastiness of the victuals.

Keogh was duly appreciative. He doubted that Curt had any real notion what he was eating, since he was clearly under a spell—the witchery of bright eyes and a ready smile. Keogh observed that he did full justice to the meal, however.

But despite the women's smiles, their underlying uneasiness was not lost on Keogh. Things on the ranch were not what they seemed on the surface.

Hendricks was a good host. He avoided any mention of cattle, or the buying or selling thereof, until they had returned outside and found chairs on the big porch on the shady side of the house. Keogh puffed appreciatively at a cigar proffered by their host; Curt had declined one with a murmur of thanks. The sun still had another hour to go, but the heat was not oppressive.

Keogh appeared to study his cigar, his mind busy on other matters. It was a long time since he'd had a weed between his teeth, and while this one was dry, it was not too bad. Hendricks had come up in the world, and Keogh observed as much.

"Yes, it's a change from life over on the Hardscrabble," Hendricks conceded. "I was able to get hold of this outfit this spring, and I brought in my own cattle."

"I suppose you'd be interested in selling those that are ready, if the price was right?"

Hendricks' laugh was a shade too ready.

"Why not? Who wouldn't, when it comes to that?"

"We represent Eastern interests," Keogh added casually. "The railroad coming will make a big difference, of course. I take it that you've got about a thousand head of cattle out there?"

Hendricks appraised him carefully. It took a good eye as well as a trained one to make so accurate an estimate merely while riding through. Apparently Keogh was what he claimed. Hendricks' memory of him was hazy.

"Around that," he conceded, "counting cows and calves."

"A nice-looking bunch," Keogh went on. "Better than I'd expected to find."

"They're not bad," Hendricks agreed, "though of course the best cattle in this whole country are on the Jackson Ranch, which adjoins this. Thoroughbred Herefords. You don't often find anything of that kind west of the river."

"That's true enough. But I don't suppose those would be for sale?"

"Not as beef animals, I'm afraid. Jackson has built up quite a herd, but he'll hold them for fancy prices for breeding stock."

"Naturally. Well, yours seem to be good beef animals. How many are ready for market—four or five hundred head?"

Curt had been listening with only half an ear, his chief attention on the sounds emanating from the kitchen, where the women were doing up the dishes. He wondered if he dared offer to help, but feared the gesture might be misunderstood—or perhaps too well understood. At any rate, an occasional gurgle of soft laughter was a pleasant sound.

He started from his reverie, coming to strained attention to what Keogh was saying.

"We might be able to offer you, say, ten thousand dollars for five hundred head of your best steers. But we wouldn't want to take delivery for several weeks— not until the railroad starts a regular service."

The son of a gun! Curt thought, torn between admiration and dismay; jingling a two-bit piece and a pair of dimes in his pocket, and talking casually of a cash deal of such proportions. Those who said of Keogh that he was half vinegar, half gall, were not wide of the mark.

Dismayed, he realized that Keogh was making at least part of this play for his benefit. Keogh was aware of Curt's sudden and deep interest in Betty, and he knew that she would not be likely to show much interest in an average cowboy; should she do so, there could be no question as to how her father would react.

Like most of his fellows, Hendricks was inclined to be democratic, but along certain rigid lines which would change only as a man's status altered. He followed certain unwritten rules, not lightly to be set aside. The fact that to begin with he'd been no more than a two-bit cowhand in his own right would only render him more adamant. No down-at-the-heels cowpoke would be good enough for *his* daughter; he knew what such a life was like.

Curt felt his ears turning pink at the trend of his thoughts. Betty seemed like a mighty nice girl, though she at times appeared nervous, almost afraid. He was afraid in turn that he could understand why. Was he really getting interested in a girl, especially the daughter of a man involved with a questionable outfit? It was suddenly a crazy mixed-up business, and so was he. Of course a girl wasn't responsible for what her dad might do along business lines—

Keogh apparently had decided the same thing; also that he liked and approved of Betty. Now he was working to give Curt a chance, if he wanted it.

Hendricks' nod was thoughtful. It struck Curt that he was more eager than he wished to appear.

"You know, that might work out and become a deal," he observed. "Cash on delivery, of course."

"Sounds like we might work something out," Keogh agreed, and stood up with a sigh.

"That was a mighty good supper," he said appreciatively. "Makes me feel as full-fed and lazy as a cat behind a stove. But we'd best be getting on. We'll have another look at the bunch as we ride through, then be back in a few days to talk business."

"That's fine," Hendricks agreed. "But you boys don't need to be in such a hurry. Be glad to have you spend the night. There's a spare room."

Mention of a spare room in the house, rather than in the bunkhouse was a distinct sign of favor. Curt sighed at Keogh's answer.

"Why, that's kind of you, but we have to keep busy," Keogh returned. Curt hid his disappointment. It would be a nice evening—especially with the right company—

Betty brought his shirt, sponged and neatly mended. They took their leave, promising to be back. Curt wondered uneasily about that. Another time, there was no telling how welcome they might be.

Hendricks rode with them among the herd, indicating the excellent quality of individual animals and the bunch as a whole. Keogh finally pulled up, staring thoughtfully into the distance where the sun had left a lingering splash against the horizon.

"We should be able to do business," he said. "We'll be back and talk things over, on the basis of what I suggested." Hendricks seemed pleased.

"See that you do that," he agreed. "I won't be the only one that'll be glad to see you boys again. So don't be too long."

Some of the glow of the evening fell away as Hendricks returned to the buildings. One of the pair who had cared for the visitors' horses was waiting for him.

"I had a look at those cayuses," he confided. "Struck me there was something a shade odd somewhere—though it took a while to figure out what it was."

A return of his earlier uneasiness gripped Hendricks like a hand feeling for his throat in the darkness. He swallowed uncomfortably.

"What do you mean?"

"What do you know about this pair—this Keogh, for instance?"

"Not much," Hendricks confessed, "though he spent a spell in this part of the country maybe five, six years back. A harmless enough sort; everybody liked him."

"Maybe it's all right. We can't be too careful,

though, these days."

An irritability born of his own apprehensions swept over Hendricks.

"If you've got something to tell me, say it," he blurted.

"Might mean something—might not. Only the horse that the young feller rode has come a long way. Hoofs worn despite shoes, and so on. Keogh's horse has no shoes, but it seems fresh, not much wear. Struck me as odd."

"Might be, might not," Hendricks conceded. "Thanks for keeping your eyes open. I'll take care of it."

He went on to the house, moving thoughtfully. By rights, he should report this to the boss, since it had a suspicious sound and might hold some significance.

On the other hand, he liked these boys—and so, clearly, did both his women-folks. They wouldn't like it if he poisoned minds against them with no real proof to back up his charges. Unhappily he shook his head.

"Well," he growled, "Keogh ain't trying to hide his name or what he's doing. Everybody can listen and make up their own minds. I got troubles enough without messin' around about a horse's hoofs!"

5.

"What now?" Curt asked. "Do we ride into Cactus Valley and bunk in a livery stable? Look sort of funny for cattle buyers."

"It might, so we won't do anything of the sort," Keogh returned. "There should be better accommodations closer at hand. You wouldn't mind bunking with a ghost, would you?"

"What sort of a ghost?" Curt demanded suspiciously. "Is it pedigreed, like those Herefords on the Jackson Ranch, or would it be just a run of the herd scrub sort of ghost?"

"Pedigreed," Keogh assured him solemnly. "Sired by the ancient red men who used to rule the roost, and damned by just about everybody. It's reasonably up to date as spooks go, and generally known these days as the ghost of old Friedland, searching, I presume, for his lost dreams."

The moon had risen, affording an uncertain light. A definite change in the landscape had become noticeable. Hill country loomed ahead, timbered and broken, but hereabouts the land was barren. From being rich and well watered, it had become dry, almost like a desert. Such grass as managed to grow was short and scanty, no longer flourishing.

A small stream prowled through the waste. Their horses halted, lowering their noses to the water, then snorted distastefully as a faintly unpleasant odor permeated the air. Somewhere ahead a dim bulk loomed, unquestionably a building, but much too big for a house or even a barn.

"This is Friedland's Folly," Keogh explained. "I don't know for sure that his ghost has a monopoly. The Indians used to give this country a wide berth, and, most everyone has followed their example—except Friedland, of course."

"What about him?" He was probably expected to find humor in the situation, but at the moment, Curt found it hard to match his companion's mood. "And what's that pile ahead there?"

"That's the Folly, and since it's stood empty for years, we shouldn't have any trouble finding room enough for the night. We may need shelter, for I have a notion there will be a shower before morning."

"What on earth is it?" Curt persisted, as the long, low building appeared more distinctly. "Why, it's huge. Who'd ever build a place like that way off here?"

"Friedland would, and did. He was a tenderfoot, fresh from the East and full of dreams when he came.

They say he intended to establish a meat-packing business, right in the heart of the cattle country. So he went ahead and built this. Hired a lot of workers; hauled in lumber, even some equipment. He didn't stop to take into consideration the distances involved, the fact he was so far from any market for his product, the lack of a railroad or other transportation, not to mention such things as refrigeration. Why he picked this spot is anybody's guess. But he acquired a thousand acres of worthless land. Paid cash for it, or that's the way the story runs."

"Even seeing it, I can't believe it," Curt protested. "Nobody would be that big a fool."

"The building's here," Keogh pointed out with irrefutable logic. "He ran out of money and confidence at about the same time, and the story is that he died of a broken heart. The building has stood, deserted, ever since. And this thousand acres of worthless land marks the boundary, on one side, of the XT, and of Jackson's spread to the north. Well, let's make ourselves at home."

They unsaddled, putting the horses on picket ropes; then Keogh led the way inside a yawning, cavernous doorway. Curt followed, not too happily. It was a shelter, and there was a threat of storm in the air; nonetheless, he would have preferred some other place to camp. The interior had a faintly musty smell, but it appeared to have been shunned and left untenanted, even by prowlers of the wilderness.

It was too dark to see much. They spread their blankets, and Curt lay wakeful, turning his thoughts to the supper they had eaten and the friendly brightness in the eyes of his hostess. Had he merely imagined that they were full of appeal, and that they also held fright? This was a strange set-up, and Keogh had not improved the atmosphere with his suggestion of ghosts. But his companion's deep breathing showed that Keogh was asleep.

Curt awoke to a crash of thunder which seemed to shake the building. He stared with wide-eyed incredulity at the thick blackness, which had been torn apart by the lightning. Had he seen something, or was that part of a dream—or a nightmare?

He was shaking all over when a second flash made the interior almost as bright as day, and this time there could be no mistake.

They were not alone in the barn-like place. Someone, or something, crouched only yards away.

Rain made a slashing assault on the roof, so drenching a downpour that Curt checked a headlong impulse to get outside. He became aware that Keogh was awake, too, and also sitting upright. As the rain subsided, the strained quality of Curt's voice startled even himself.

"Did you see something, Keogh?"

"I'm afraid I did," Keogh conceded, and all levity was gone from his voice. There was more thunder as he spoke, and another vivid flash of lightning. Keogh's leveled gun was in his hand. Curt discovered that it was a man who sat, his back to the opposite wall, or at least what had once been a man. Then the darkness closed in again.

There was a soft click as the hammer of Keogh's revolver eased off from full cock. Keogh's voice was calm once more.

"Whoever he is, he's long past doing anyone any harm. The poor devil must have come in here to die."

There was no more thunder, just a continuing downpour, until the rain gradually lessened; then only the dripping of the eaves remained. Keogh's even breathing showed that he had gone back to sleep. That was probably the sensible thing, but not easy to accomplish.

They had failed to notice the huddled figure when spreading their blankets in the gloom. Probably he had been there for a long while, some wayfaring pilgrim who had sought shelter—and had remained. Friedland's Folly. A place shunned by red men and white alike, long before the tenderfoot had built this monstrosity of a packing shed.

A lively imagination could be uncomfortable. Convinced that he would get no more sleep that night, Curt awoke at daylight to find Keogh tugging on his boots.

Curt's eyes turned instinctively to the farther wall. It had been no trick of the light, no figment of their imagination. The man was there, sitting with legs outstretched before him, his back to the wall, an old black hat tipped down, covering most of the face. Keogh crossed and examined him curiously. At his sharply indrawn breath, Curt bounced to his feet, clutching one boot.

"What's wrong?" he asked. Outside, sunshine was across the land, but this monstrous room seemed dank and close.

"Looks like plenty was wrong," Keogh returned, his voice suddenly grim. He had tipped back the hat, then allowed it to drop in place again. "I used to know this man." He struck an attitude. "Alas, poor Yorick!"

"Looks like an Indian," Curt observed doubtfully. "And he's been here for quite a spell—judging by appearances."

"Quite a while," Keogh agreed. "He's a Pawnee. Runs Like a Wolf. From the look of things, one time he didn't run fast enough."

"What do you mean?"

Keogh indicated a small hole in the back of the coat, barely visible as the dead man sat there. Such a hole could only have been made by a bullet.

"Murder," Keogh said tightly. "Shot in the back. He must have lived awhile, long enough to get this far. Maybe he figured it was a place of refuge, where others wouldn't follow. Or perhaps he was just looking for shelter. He came in, sat down—and never got up again."

An eerie quality clung to the place, despite the daylight. Keogh's logical summary served to alleviate it only in part.

"Let's get going," Curt suggested. "There's nothing we can do for him—and I'm hungry again. You figure our reputation as cattle buyers would make our credit good for a pair of breakfasts, once we reach town?"

Keogh did not reply. He turned from the dead man to an examination of the huge, barn-like room. Viewed by daylight, it was clear that the place had been visited since being abandoned by its builder. Considerable planking had been ripped away at one end, probably by someone in need of lumber. A few tools had been left behind, including a shovel. Keogh picked it up.

"He was a pretty good Indian," he said quietly, "and I counted him as a friend. About the least we can do is bury him. He must have been here the better part of a year, maybe longer, and nobody's been around in all that time."

Curt opened his mouth to demur, thought better of it, and shrugged. Once Keogh made up his mind to a course, he was difficult to dissuade.

"Show me where, and I'll do the digging," Curt offered, "if you'll tend to the other part."

"That's fair enough," Keogh agreed. They stepped outside, and the air seemed washed and clean. There the freshness ended. Curt tasted the sparkling creek water, finding it as unpleasant as on the day before.

"No wonder nothing will come around this place," he observed disgustedly. "It tastes terrible—sulphur and iron, maybe. Friedland must have been really crazy to pick such a place."

Keogh found a spot, wet from the night's rain, which was less rocky than most. As Curt dug, he returned to the building.

They buried Runs Like a Wolf, and Curt, moved by impulse, picked a few wild flowers and placed them on the grave.

"Now do we get going?" he asked.

"Might as well," Keogh agreed. "First we'll take something to jingle in our pockets," he added, and showed Curt an old wooden box set back in another corner of the big room. It had been partially hidden by a collection of refuse, and was so rotted that it was commencing to fall apart.

Keogh had pried loose a board, revealing that inside the box were iron washers, the size of silver dollars. Some appeared rusted, but most were still bright. Apparently they had been part of the original supplies for the packing plant, which had never been used.

Keogh took a double handful, but Curt disdained them. "If they were dollars, and spendable, I'd use some." He sighed. "But those would be just so much dead weight."

They swung west, and a couple of hours of steady riding brought them to the town. Cactus Valley drowsed in the sun like a somnolent hound, and seemed a fair replica of the average cow town. The Army post, Keogh explained, lay half a dozen miles east by north.

Curt had a sense of unseen eyes watching as they rode in; a hard and suspicious scrutiny. If Keogh felt it, he gave no sign, heading straight for the livery barn and riding in through the wide standing doors. A stable boy appeared as he swung down.

"Give our horses a good rub-down," Keogh instructed, "and a feed of oats. We'll likely be staying for a few days."

Curt smiled feebly. "Sounds as though our cayuses will eat better than we do." He sighed.

"We'll eat," Keogh promised. "But everything in order." There was one hotel, and the fading sign proclaimed it to be the Palace House.

"Under the circumstances, the best there is is none too good for us," Keogh observed jauntily, and led the way. He explained that they wanted a room. The clerk, in whom the milk of human kindness appeared to have curdled, pushed forward a frayed ledger.

"Rooms are a dollar a night," he observed pointedly, and waited.

Keogh signed with a flourish. "The usual price." He nodded, and tugged out a red leather purse. The last time Curt had seen it, the pocketbook had been as limp as he felt without his breakfast. Now it bulged, catching in the pocket. Keogh tugged impatiently, and it came loose and thudded to the floor.

There was a solid, reassuring clink. Keogh scooped it up and returned it to his pocket, but the clerk's suspicious eyes had taken on a look of respect.

"This is for you, a small emolument for services rendered," Keogh murmured, and tossed their lone two-bit piece carelessly on the desk. The clerk moved briskly, climbing the stairs, throwing open a door, indicating the iron bedstead from which paint was flaking, the single chair and a washstand with a cracked mirror above.

"This is our best, gents," he explained. "I hope you'll find it to be what you want."

"It should do for our sojourn in your midst." Keogh shrugged. "We'll probably have to stay around for several days."

"In that case, the rate's five dollars a week."

"What are those ventilations in the wall and ceiling?" Keogh asked suspiciously. "Bullet holes?"

"Why, yeah. I guess they are," the clerk admitted apologetically. "That happened a long while ago. The trouble with that particular gent was, he'd had a few drinks too many. Got to imaginin' that he saw bed-b— uh, flies on the ceiling, and tried to shoot them. We don't often have characters like that."

"I hope his imagination wasn't based on bites," Keogh returned pointedly. "It was our impression that this was supposed to be a high-class hostelry."

"Well, I wouldn't know none about a thing like that, but it's a good hotel," the clerk assured him earnestly. "We don't tolerate bugs. I'm sure you'll like it."

He retreated down the stairs, then ducked through a side door into the adjoining saloon. The cavernous-faced proprietor had been awaiting his coming, being both owner of the saloon and landlord of the Palace. "Well?" he asked.

"Here's how they registered." The clerk tendered the ledger. "They're kind of particular."

"Hm." Pratt studied the signature. "Don't mean anything. They pay in advance?"

"Not yet, but he has a purse bulgin' with money. Give me a two-bit tip."

Pratt's nearly lidless eyes brightened. "In that case, it don't matter," he said softly. "Whether they're small fry or big fish—we will find out."

6.

Curt looked about the room, testing the mattress doubtfully.

"Feels like a relief map of the Rocky Mountains," he observed. "The dirt floor we had last night was softer. But I suppose we can stand it. You think you can keep stallin' him? You did make good use of those old washers."

"They clink convincingly," Keogh agreed. "Let's look over the town."

"I'd like to look over a plate full of ham and eggs," Curt responded wistfully. They strolled down the street, pacing resolutely past a restaurant through whose open door wafted odors which, if less delectable than those of the previous evening, were still tantalizing. A man emerged, allowing the screen door to slam behind him, picking at his teeth with a silver toothpick. He blinked, then exclaimed incredulously: "Keogh, as I'm a sinner! Why, you old horse thief, you, who let you out of jail?"

Keogh swung about, then grinned. The next instant the two were pummeling each other joyously.

"Fred Whipple!" Keogh marveled. "You still clutterin' up the scenery? I figured they'd have lynched you years ago!"

"I guess likely they was short of rope," Whipple explained. He was a portly figure whose hair was beginning to gray, giving him a look of dignity and substance belied by his dress and air. "Man, Keogh, you're a sight for sore eyes. Must be all of five years since you rode this way last. What are you doing for yourself these days?"

"We're cattle buyers," Keogh explained carelessly. "Heard about the Jackson Ranch, and others in the neighborhood, and stopped on our way on West. This is my partner, Curt Conners."

Whipple shook hands, his eyes envious. "Cattle buyers!" he repeated. "I always knew you'd do big things, Keogh. Not that you'll be likely to have much luck at Jackson's. He don't aim to sell for ordinary beef. But Hendricks has a nice herd, for one."

"We looked at his bunch yesterday. Some good beef there."

"Ain't nothin' wrong with the meat on the hoof—it's countin' them that gets tricky." Whipple chuckled. "Ask the major out at the post—only be ready to duck when you do, for that's a plumb touchy subject with him. But come along and have a drink. There's a couple of the boys in town that you'll remember—Zeke Tone and Tom O'Malley."

He led the way into the saloon, where they found Tone and O'Malley listlessly indulging in a game of cards. The reunion was warm. Clearly Keogh was remembered, and favorably.

Zeke was a scarecrow figure, badly bowed legs adding to the effect. He slapped a thigh in sudden recollection.

"Maybe Keogh can help us out with what we need to know," he said. "You remember Abernathy, Keogh?"

Keogh nodded without hesitation. "Of course," he agreed. "Whatever else you might say about him, Abernathy wasn't easy to overlook. What about him?"

"Well, it's this way," Zeke explained. "We sort of need to be able to produce him—in a manner of speakin'—and now we find that he ain't exactly available."

"Which is hardly to be wondered at, considering that he's been buried now for quite a spell of years," Keogh pointed out.

"Yeah, that's one of the difficulties," Tone admitted. "And I guess I might as well set the record straight by admittin' that I've kind of bungled matters, though I did so with the best of intentions. But you tell him, Fred. You're better at explainin' than I am."

Whipple nodded agreeably. "The fix we all sort of find ourselves involved in started when Zeke here got a letter in the mail. That was sev'ral months ago now. It surprised him to the point where he didn't quite know whether he was him, or some other feller."

"Well, that was the first letter I'd had in going

on ten years," Zeke explained apologetically.

"Anyhow, the letter was from a lady, way back in the state of Noo Jersey," Whipple went on. "She was, according to the signature, no less a person than Mrs. George Abernathy. First time that any of us had ever known about Abernathy havin' a wife back East."

Keogh nodded. "I never heard of that," he acknowledged. "But it's not too surprising—considering."

"No, I reckon not. Well, it seems that somehow this Mrs. Abernathy had heard about Zeke—somebody returned East from a trip out this way and recollected the name—so she up and wrote Zeke a letter. Said she understood that Zeke had been a friend of her husband out here, so she was desirous of obtainin' information concernin' same. Did Zeke know where this strayed but ever-lovin' husband of hers might be? If so, that was the information which she'd appreciate, and would he be so kind as to let her know?"

"Well, what could a man do?" Tone asked defensively. "That matter of being a friend of his was sort of too moot to argue, and you cain't just write back and inform a lady that, in addition to being a widow instead of a wife, she's lucky to be one, said strayin' husband havin' been a horse thief, among other things. Anyway, I didn't know too much about it, Keogh. You was the one who knew better'n anybody else about him. Not knowin' where you might be, though, I answered her as well as I could, informin' her that he'd sort of demised a spell ago, and sympathizin' with the grief she'd no doubt feel. Seemed like that was the least I could do."

"The trouble was, she wanted more than that," Whipple took up the thread again. "I don't reckon that the news of his demise was too much of a shock to the lady, since she hadn't seen him for going on fifteen years, and hadn't even heard from him for most of that time. Anyway, she wrote right back and sort of let on that the business he'd left behind him when he'd headed West had done a whole lot better after he was out of the way—which ain't greatly to be wondered at."

All four men nodded. Curt could get the picture. Abernathy had clearly been more of a debit than a credit, both as a man and as a husband.

"She explained that the business had done right well, so she was well fixed. That being so, she wanted to have a marker placed on the grave of the late lamented—a living marker; no less than a red rose-bush. And would Zeke, as an old friend of her husband, be so good as to undertake such a chore? She would ship the bush out here, and he was to plant it in the proper place, for which service she would pay well."

Zeke nodded defensively, plucking nervously at a sparse mustache.

"By then I'd sort of got myself into a box," he

explained, "innocently allowin', in my letters, that I knew all about Abernathy and his whereabouts. Anyway, if such a harmless but touchin' piece of information would bring heart balm to the lady, what was wrong with it? Seemed to be the least a man could do."

"Zeke's intentions was as lily-white as the driven snow," Whipple agreed. "But it sort of created a misunderstandin'. Without no further dilly-dallyin' or correspondence from this end, Mrs. Abernathy sends word that she's shippin' the rosebush for plantin', along with a money order for a hundred dollars to pay him for his trouble. And of course, Zeke being Zeke, he can use the money. But the trouble, as it turns out, is that none of us remembers where old Abernathy was planted—providin' we ever knew, of which we ain't too sure."

Keogh pondered, scratching an ear reflectively. "She was sure that he'd remained a lovin' husband to the end?"

Zeke Tone's nod was positive. "Her faith in that no-good yahoo was so touchin', I couldn't nowise bear to shake it."

Curt observed a heavy-set man dismounting and tying his horse at a rail across the street. The fellow was as heavily whiskered as he had been a day or so earlier, and he looked about furtively. Curt came back to the story.

"And now she's sendin' a rosebush to be planted

above Abernathy's grave?" Keogh added.

"She sure is. Zeke got another letter yesterday, sayin' it would arrive any day now. Which presents a problem."

"Meaning that you can't plant it where it's supposed to be, not knowing the location of said grave?"

"That's what it boils down to, and it seems a shame. But maybe you recall where the old coot's planted?"

"I might, but again I might not," Keogh conceded. "I've taken part in a number of funerals, one time and another. I'd have to give some thought to it. It's been quite a while."

The heavy-set man entered the saloon almost defiantly, shouldering up to the bar. No one took much notice.

"Yeah, it sure has." Whipple shrugged. "But as I recollect, it was you who helped bury him—assisted in said chore by Cactus Pete and a Pawnee buck named Runs Like a Wolf."

Keogh eyed him admiringly, while Curt's attention sharpened at the name. "That's right. You've a good memory, Fred."

"I hope you have," Whipple grunted. "Cactus has been reposin' peaceful in Boot Hill most of the time since, due to an argument concernin' the Ace of Clubs. And nobody's seen hide nor hair of the Pawnee for going on a year now, which seems to leave you as the sole custodian of the information of where said restin' place is at."

7.

Thoughtfully Keogh rubbed an ear, but his question seemed rather far afield.

"We caught a far glimpse of Friedland's Folly as we rode along," he said. "Building's still standing, looks like. That's sure a lonely sort of place. Who owns it now, does anybody know?"

Curt, tightening his belt an additional notch, observed the sudden attention with which Pratt, behind the bar, seemed to listen, Zeke's face brightened. Here was a mistake other than his own. He gestured toward Pratt.

"Mister Pratt, Keogh here wants to know who owns the Folly these days."

The question did nothing to relieve Pratt's normally doleful cast of countenance.

"Go on; rub it in," he grunted. "I reckon I'm the goat, Mister Keogh. I took that land one time on a gamblin' debt, and in winning, I sure turned out to be the loser."

"A big debt?" Keogh suggested.

"Three hundred dollars, it was. And that feller had had the nerve to play with me without a cent in his pocket!"

"But a thousand acres of land, such as it is," Keogh murmured. He eyed Pratt thoughtfully. Though tending his own bar, Pratt was obviously the owner. He might not be adverse to some betting on the side.

"What sort of a game was it?"

"Dice." Pratt shrugged. "I got no time for nothing slower than that." He eyed the newcomers thoughtfully, remembering the clerk's report of a heavily filled purse. "Maybe you'd care to roll a few?"

Keogh yawned and stretched. "I might, at that," he acknowledged. "Something to break the monotony."

Pratt was already untying his apron and tossing it to a horse-faced assistant, who materialized as if on cue from a back room. He produced a pair of dice like a conjuring trick, settling into a chair at a table, straddling it, hairy arms resting over the back. He was suddenly eager, and Curt caught the dismay in the eyes of the other men, the veiled warnings in their faces as they looked at Keogh.

"Count me out," Whipple stated, scraping back his own chair. "I got to be getting along."

"So've we," O'Malley remembered, and Tone was only a step behind.

"We're late as it is. See you around, Keogh."

Pratt laughed. He was transformed, rough and

swaggering, sure of himself. "This'll just be a few throws between the two of us," he announced. "Something to break the monotony, like you say." His eyes filmed like those of a hawk. "I like to see betting money on the table before I begin," he added pointedly.

"Good idea," Keogh agreed. "I'm that way myself." He thrust a hand into his pocket, then frowned as it came out empty.

"Curt, will you oblige me by stepping across to our room and fetching my money belt?" he asked. "That or my purse. I'll have to get some change."

"Sure; glad to," Curt agreed. He understood he was supposed to take his time about the errand, in view of the fact there was no money belt. He hesitated, uneasy. The others had gone, clearly wanting no part in any game with the owner of the saloon. Keogh would be alone. But he usually knew what he was doing.

"We can wait, if you like," Keogh said, with an indifferent shrug. "Plenty of time."

Pratt hesitated, but Keogh's play was convincing. These men were cattle buyers, and they had money. And if it turned out to be otherwise—

"No need for that," Pratt decided. He tossed the dice to the middle of the table. "You first. We can start at ten dollars, or what would you prefer?"

"That suits me," Keogh agreed, and closed long fingers over the cubes. His shake was slow and easy, his attitude indifferent, nor did his face show even a faint trace of emotion as he won. "Maybe we should double?"

Pratt nodded, intent and wordless. When Curt finally returned, his face was sweaty, his breathing heavy as if from a hard run. Keogh still lounged, as indifferent as ever.

"That makes five hundred," he announced. "Shall we call it a day, or try another whirl?"

Pratt was torn between caution and avarice. It was clear that he was not accustomed to losing, and the temptation to continue play was strong. One good roll could wipe out his debt. The difficulty was that another bad turn of the dice would double it.

"Tell you what," Keogh suggested amiably. "I'll give you a chance to get your money back, and risk nothing. I'll stack that five hundred I've won against the deed to Friedland's Folly. Gives you a chance to double on that, too," he added, and his grin was disarming.

Pratt's breathing subsided to a slow wheeze; his eyes were darting and suspicious. That he was tempted was clear, but Keogh had been having a run of luck, and there was more here than met the eye. Curt was back, waiting expectantly. The big Colt's which sagged in Keogh's worn holster looked as competent as the man who wore it.

What he had to do hurt like pulling a tooth, alleviated only by the reflection that this was merely the first round in their game. Slowly, Pratt shook his head.

"I guess not," he decided. "We've had our fun," he added heavily. "But if it goes beyond that, it ain't so much fun." Slowly he counted out the money to pay his account and shoved it across the table. "Gives you some small change," he gibed.

"Why, so it does," Keogh agreed, and stuffed the money carelessly into a pocket. He arose, stretching again. "From the looks of the sun, Curt, it's about time to eat," he observed, and Curt followed outside in awed tribute. Not until steaks had been set before them did he break the silence.

"You sure haven't lost your touch, Keogh. I didn't really think you could shake out such a string."

"I was shaking in my boots," Keogh confided gravely. They returned to the Palace, to find the clerk slouched behind the desk. He rolled his eyes at them speculatively. The ledger lay open.

Keogh took the hint. He pulled a handful of coins from his pocket and carelessly tossed five dollars on the desk.

"We'll pay for a week in advance," he explained, and neither of them missed the avarice in the look which followed them as they climbed the stairs.

"Gives one the feel of walking in a nest of rattlesnakes," Curt observed as he closed the door. He eyed the latch sharply. "No key," he added. "And seeing we're so suddenly cluttered with wealth, a good lock could be nice to have."

Keogh shrugged. "That lock has long since out-grown its key." Opening his hand, he tossed a pair of dice onto the bed. "There's the answer," he said. "Pratt contributed these, too—though he didn't know it."

Observing how they had fallen, Curt picked them up, shook them and tossed them down. Once more the pattern was unmistakable.

"Loaded, eh?"

"If a six-gun could be set up on the same principle, you'd be able to shoot a thousand times," Keogh agreed. "They're fixed to come up seven or eleven more regular than the rising sun. That sometimes runs into a cloudy day."

"But if Pratt had this loaded pair—"

"A loaded gun don't always shoot straight. He was too eager. An expert can spoil the roll if he wants to—not that Pratt would be likely to bother about such details. I had a pair of straight dice in my pocket, and since they were the same size and color, we played with those. By now, he will likely have figured out what happened."

"You left yours in place of these?"

"Seemed like a fair trade, considerin'."

Curt stared at him thoughtfully. "What do we do now?"

"I was thinking we might ride out and make a friendly call at the fort; pay our respects to the major."

Pratt's scowl dissolved to a thoughtful glumness as he studied the dice in his hand. A few throws, within the privacy of the back room which he called his office, had failed to explain Keogh's run of luck, but it made his own lack of success understandable.

"The dirty so and so!" he observed. "Substitutin' these, right under my nose, and beating me at my own game!" He swept them out of sight as a knock sounded; then the stable boy entered.

"They took their horses just now and rode out," he reported. "I thought you'd like to know."

Pratt's face had a suddenly frosty look, as he remembered his five hundred dollars which had gone with them. He collapsed suddenly into a chair.

"Where did they say they was headin' for?" he gasped.

"They asked the way out to the fort," the stable boy explained. "I heard them sayin' something between themselves to the effect that the Army might be in the market for some beef."

Pratt's breathing eased, but suspicion flared higher in his eyes.

"I'd like to know more about that pair," he observed. "You keep your eyes open."

"I been doing that already. That's what I come to talk about. One horse has come a long way. Its hoofs are worn down. The other seems fresh."

Pratt stared. There had been no report by the pair assigned to keep a watch; apparently they had passed the two pards as harmless. However, Keogh had been in that country before, and Pratt was a man who played hunches. His hunch now was that something was wrong.

"Anything else?" he wheezed.

"That's all. I just thought you'd like to know."

"I do." He nodded slowly. "Be ready tonight."

8.

Major Yancey Tombright had been a fighting man all his days. He had taken it almost as a personal affront when the red tribesmen had permitted themselves to be pacified, posing no further problem. Was a soldier to do no more than twiddle his thumbs?

He looked up, not bothering to rise, scowling over a formidable brush of mustache, as the newcomers were admitted. Their appearance he found disappointing. These were not the sort of men he'd expected or hoped for, men who might be expected to get results. Keogh's appearance in particular was discouraging. He looked as imaginative as a sheep, and about as dashing as a rabbit in a patch of clover.

"I want action," he growled, once the formalities had been indulged in. He struck the desk with a bunched fist. "Darn it, it's an outrage when the United States Government is robbed and nothing is done about it!"

Disregarding the fact that they had been left to stand, Keogh draped himself carelessly across a corner of the desk. His grin was mocking.

"I understood there was a lot of action, with most of the garrison riding to and fro, like the devil seeking what he might devour," he returned, and a shade of respect crept into the major's eyes. "Exactly what did happen?"

"All that I know is that the herd was stolen out from under our very noses, the night after it was delivered," Tombright admitted. "It was snowing hard, and two of our sentries were tied up by masked men. The herd simply disappeared. No trace was ever found—at least none that amounted to anything," he added grudgingly.

"Meaning?" Keogh prodded.

Tombright hesitated, but reticence was not his strong point.

"A herd of the same size and appearance turns up on the same ranch," he blurted, "wearing a new brand, that could have been altered, with a new man running the place. I say it's darned suspicious!"

Curt listened miserably. This was what he had feared—Hendricks was apparently implicated in the stealing. Not that he cared particularly about their host of the previous afternoon. But Betty Hendricks was different.

"You're charging Hendricks with stealing the herd?" Keogh asked.

"I'm not such a fool, when I can furnish no proof," the major admitted. "But I want something done. The

Army can go just so far. Beyond that, howls of outrage would drown out a pack of yapping coyotes. But I expect you to do something." Curiously, he was beginning to feel that perhaps this man might.

"You think that Hendricks is heading up this rustling?"

Tombright snorted. "I do not! He may be one of a gang—probably he is—but he's not the boss. There's something big in the air. Stealing from the army was only part of it," he added grudgingly.

"You have your suspicions, at least?"

"Suspicion is not proof. If I named names, with nothing to back my guess, I'd merely be leading you astray."

"You're extremely helpful," Keogh retorted, and brought a flush to the major's close-shaven cheeks. "What do you know about Pratt?"

"I know I'd like to hang him," Tombright said venomously. "Selling rot gut to my men—" He broke off, controlling himself with an effort. "Maybe I'm prejudiced, but there's no love lost between us. Pratt served a hitch in the Army—or part of one. I had the misfortune to have him in my command. I cashiered him for cowardice and dereliction of duty—the only charges which could be proven. Naturally, there's no love lost between us."

"You figure he's back of all this trouble?"

"Good Lord, no. He hasn't the brains for anything as big as this."

"But maybe the will," Keogh murmured. He stood up. "It has been a pleasure to meet you, sir."

Yancey Tombright hesitated, then heaved himself erect from his chair. He thrust out a hand.

"I deserve that," he conceded. "Maybe I was mistaken in you, gentlemen. If I can render any assistance, call on me."

Darkness was doing its best to conceal man's improvements upon the face of nature when they came out after eating their supper. Since it was still early, they turned toward Pratt's saloon, there being nothing else to do in Cactus Valley.

The heavy-set, whiskered man whom they had noticed earlier in the day was seated by himself at a table in a corner, a half-emptied bottle beside him. To this he had recourse at intervals, staring at the other customers with a look both challenging and defiant.

It was only when the bottle was empty, and he called for another, that Pratt's obvious uneasiness came to the fore. He crossed to the table, explaining, apparently arguing. The climax came swiftly.

The big man was drunk, though apparently not as drunk as he wished to be. He heaved himself suddenly to his feet, upsetting the table, sending the empty bottle crashing, reaching unsteadily for Pratt. More by chance than by design, his pawing grab closed on Pratt's holstered revolver, and the next instant he was shooting wildly.

A hanging lamp shattered, followed by the reek of coal-oil, but fortunately there was no flash of flame. Pratt and three or four others closed around him, and with a roar, the bearded man went into action. In such a mood he was like a berserk bull, and the whole room was instantly in an uproar. The remaining lamp went out.

Not feeling that this was his fight, Curt prudently retreated, only to stagger and almost lose his balance as a hurtling body surged against him. He grabbed instinctively to save himself, and something came loose in his hand. There was a further smash of breaking glass as a window went out, and Curt, reaching the door, let himself out into the night. He was relieved to find Keogh beside him.

Only when they had reached their own room and lit a lamp was Curt able to survey the trophy which had come loose in his hand. He had already guessed what it was, but he surveyed it with increasing amazement. It was a set of false whiskers.

"And they're the ones that fellow was wearing," he commented. "They pulled loose when I got hold of them by chance. Now what would he want to wear those for?"

Keogh examined the beard thoughtfully. "It's handmade," he pointed out. "Part of a horse's mane, I'd guess. And rather a good job, on the whole." He handed it back, then tugged off a boot and dropped it with a resounding thud.

"I hope you aren't sleepy," he said. Having dropped the other shoe with an equal thump, he picked the boots up softly. "Let's move to the next room. The others are empty, and when it comes time, I'd like to get a good night's sleep."

Pratt had been busy. Contrary to the major's opinion, he possessed talents which ordinarily were not displayed to the world at large. Uneasy despite himself, he despatched a messenger to the Two Diamond I, but no answer could be expected for some hours. Even when it came, it might prove meaningless.

He was in an increasingly troubled frame of mind, following the unceremonious departure of the bearded man via a window. The fellow had given them the slip in the darkness, and for the present there was nothing to be done about it.

Something could be done, however, without waiting for others. He hastened the hour of closing by hustling a remaining pair of customers to the street without apology. The bartender was despatched for the stable boy, who arrived promptly. Pratt gave a partial explanation to the pair.

"We've a little chore to do—and it could turn out to be profitable, providin' this Keogh has a money belt or a loaded purse, like he says."

The bartender was inclined to squint, and at the mention of money he actually became cross-eyed.

"You figure he might?"

"The way he gallops those dominoes, he just might," Pratt agreed. "Walk soft."

They crossed through the side door into the hotel, where the heavy-lidded clerk gave no indication of having stirred or changed position since Keogh and Curt had climbed the stairs to the second floor. He exhibited no surprise at sight of the trio, with Pratt at their head. The saloonkeeper gestured with a jerk of his head.

"They in their room?"

"Yeah. Asleep since an hour ago, I reckon."

"They figured to make a fool of me," Pratt explained matter-of-factly, and had no need to point out how heinous was such an offense. "The ladder handy?"

"Right where you left it the last time."

Pratt dipped long fingers into a coat pocket and extracted a collection of dark-colored bandanas. One of these he adjusted over his face; it was held in position by his hat. The others he distributed to his assistants, who accepted them casually.

"You two get the ladder and get up to the window," Pratt instructed. "Listen for us coming in at the door. And no shooting, unless it's necessary."

He waited a couple of minutes after the two had gone out into the night, then led the way, moving with the ease of long familiarity. The clerk followed, reaching a revolver from the drawer of the desk and dropping it into a pocket. Halfway up the stairs he grunted in caution.

"Watch that next step. It squeaks."

"I remember it," Pratt assured him, and set his weight gingerly at the extreme edge. "By rights, I ought to kill him, pullin' a trick like that on me," he grunted. "Maybe I will anyhow." He halted, hand on the door knob. "You ready?"

There was a repressed eagerness in the reply: "Lead the way!"

Keogh occupied the single straight-backed chair; he had been sitting silent and expectant for the last hour, tipped back against the wall. Curt, stretched on the bed but tensely wakeful, heard the faint creek of the stairs, the soft thud of a ladder as it was dropped against the side of the building, below a window. He came off the bed without a sound.

"They hold us lightly," Keogh observed in a whisper. "Another couple of hours, and we could be expected to be in a much deeper sleep."

He peered from a crack of the door. "Masks seem to be in order," he added, and adjusted his own bandana beneath his hat. Curt followed suit, his heart thudding so that he wondered if the others might hear. Despite having worked often with Keogh, he could never quite adjust to his unorthodox ways.

The door to the next room, which had been assigned them, opened soundlessly. Keogh had observed that the hinges on every door were well-oiled, also that the window, which lacked a screen, moved more smoothly than was customary for hotel windows.

A pair of shadowy figures were slipping into the room, and Keogh joined them, Curt at his heels. A hulking mass was darkening the window, making the transfer from the ladder with surprising grace and stealth. The room seemed full of ghosts.

"All right!" Pratt's voice was not loud, but its harsh stridency was as sharp as a newly-honed bowie. "Come awake, and don't make no fuss!"

9.

Only a dim light entered by the door and window, picking up faint gleams along the nickelplating of gun barrels. Since the guns in Keogh's and Curt's hands were of blued steel, they gave back no visible reflection.

Nothing moved; there was no creak of the bed or startled motion of men rudely awakened. Someone breathed heavily. Pratt cursed beneath his breath.

"Now what the devil—"

"Take it easy, boys." Keogh's voice had a somewhat disembodied effect. "Nothing to get excited about—if you do as we say! First, let go of your guns. Let them drop."

Time pulsated like a throbbing artery, and one man tried a sudden move of desperation. He cried out as Curt's gun barrel chopped on his wrist, and the gun clattered on the bare floor boards. There was another interval, in which tension built agonizingly. Keogh did not repeat the warning, but the click was audible as he eared back the hammer of his gun. The others let go of their weapons.

"That's better," Keogh commended them softly. "Now see if you can hold up the ceiling. Don't let it drop, for heavy, heavy hangs over your poor heads! Only you, there by the stand, light the lamp."

For a third time there was a delay, while the bartender calculated his chances of going for a hide-out gun, then abandoned the notion. It was impossible to pick a target in the gloom, and the risk was too great.

A match scratched, the flame hot against the blackness. It dwindled to a faint flare, then ran raggedly along the lamp wick. Light blossomed as the chimney was replaced.

"Fine," Keogh approved. He felt each man for additional weapons, while Curt stood with his back to the door, eyes gleaming through slits in his own mask.

"I suppose we should feel complimented, the way you come out as if against an army," Keogh observed. "I didn't realize that we were that important. And speaking of coming out, how about coming out from under cover?"

Again there was hesitation, but the guns were convincing. The hotel clerk was the first to comply. Then the others followed, Pratt being last. Keogh glimpsed the wild hatred in his eyes before he could school his face to show its usual placidity.

"Aren't they a handsome bunch of would-be bandits, Curt?" Keogh asked. "But I suppose it was all intended to be among friends, eh? Really, you boys should know better. We didn't bring our money belts into town. It occurred to us that that might not be exactly the proper thing."

He was swinging his revolver in an arc, twirling it with a finger in the trigger guard. The others watched in fascination.

"You can have your guns back in the morning," he added abruptly. "Better put the ladder back—where you can find it another time."

They eyed him, hesitating between disbelief and dawning hope, then, seeing that he meant it, took a hasty departure. But there was no gratitude or appreciation in the set face of the saloonkeeper. Keogh braced the chair back against the door and blew out the light.

Encountering Fred Whipple, Zeke Tone and Tom O'Malley after a leisurely breakfast Curt noted that the others eyed them with uneasiness.

"Sounds like you fellows must be packin' a couple of rabbits' feet apiece," Whipple observed. "But you're sure temptin' trouble, Keogh. This country ain't exactly the peaceful spot it used to be, when we didn't have nothing more'n an occasional horse thief to trouble us."

"Now you know better than that, Fred," Keogh protested. "You know that I'm peacefully inclined. There's nothing I like better than peace."

"Yeah, you like it so well that you're ready to fight for it, any time," Whipple retorted. "Don't say I didn't warn you."

"What are you fellows doing?" Keogh sought to change the subject. "You struck it rich, or something? You seem to be taking it easy, these days."

"We're takin' it easy, but strikin' it rich we ain't done." Tone sighed. "We used to work for Cole Jackson, but he laid us off. Right now we're between jobs, as you might say."

"We better be meeting the stage," O'Malley added nervously. "You need to pick up that rosebush while it's still middlin' fresh, Zeke."

"Yeah, that's so," Tone conceded, leading the way. "Latest word is that it'll be along today," he added. "I'm glad you're here, Keogh. Like Tom says, that rose 'll need plantin' as soon as possible, and you're the only one able to guide us to the right place."

The stage swung into town, then halted with a flourish. A drummer alighted, followed by a cowboy, then a lady of bold mien and attire. Last came a tiny little figure, bonneted and shawled, protectively clutching an over-large pot. In it was unmistakably a rose. Zeke moved forward, greeting her with a sweeping flourish of his hat.

"Ma'am," he observed, "welcome to our fair land. I take it that you're the custodian of Mrs. Abernathy's rose. In that case I stand ready to relieve you of said burden, me being Zeke Tone, with whom she's been correspondin' concernin' same."

Gentle brown eyes lifted searchingly to his own. Apparently the inspection was satisfactory, for with a sigh of relief the plant was relinquished to him.

"I'm pleased to greet you, Mr. Tone. As you say, here it is. Treat it gently, Mr. Tone. Land sakes, I never dreamed a plant could turn out to be more bother than a young 'un, but in some ways it has been. Travelin' near two thousand miles with it gets to be a chore. But I've kept it well watered and fresh, and now it's full of buds almost ready to bloom. I'm Jennie Abernathy," she added briskly. "I came along to watch it planted, in loving memory, over the grave of my dear husband."

Zeke all but dropped the pot. His jaw threatened to become unhinged.

"You—do you mean to say, ma'am, that you—that you're Mrs. Abernathy?" he gasped. "Why, I hadn't no idea that you aimed to come way out here yourself."

"Neither did I, Mr. Tone; neither did I," Mrs. Abernathy confessed. "Somehow the idea of traveling so far had never occurred to me. And then, all at once, the notion struck me like an inspiration. Why should I not look upon the last resting place of my dear departed? Travel would be an experience, certainly broadening, somewhat educational, perhaps even delightful. At the same time, I could make sure that the rose received the best of care on the journey.

So here I am," she added briskly. "And the journey has been, in many ways, an experience."

"I'll bet it has." Zeke's eyes threatened to cross, as always in moments of stress. He goggled uncertainly. "This is kind of a surprise," he added feebly.

"No doubt it is. I still find myself somewhat surprised. Now shall we complete the task without delay, Mr. Tone?"

"Uh, why—sure, ma'am, certainly." He tugged at an ear lobe, searching for inspiration. "Only, it's quite a way from here, Mrs. Abernathy—quite a few miles to the spot, and no road in between. So likely you'll want to rest a spell first—"

"It's thoughtful and sweet of you to be concerned about me, Mr. Tone, but I'm already toughened— I'm sure that's the word—to the hardships of the road. It is my hope, my wish, to have this rosebush planted as a living marker above the grave of my dear husband before the sun goes down."

Zeke looked at Keogh, who had been doing some fast thinking behind the usual impassive smile. He gave a slight but reassuring nod. Zeke agreed without further hesitation.

"Then what you want, ma'am, is what we'll do," he declared. "I reckon we can cover the most of the way in a buckboard, though maybe we'll have to take to saddles for the last couple of miles or so."

Whipple stepped forward helpfully, hat in hand.

"Me and some of the boys 'll ride along, if you

don't mind, Zeke," he offered. "Make sort of an escort, as you might say, in honor of this lovin' act concernin' the late departed."

Curt sensed both the real and the hidden motive behind the offer. Their presence would enable Keogh to act as guide for the party without appearing to do so. But there was more here than met the eye. It was clear that Whipple and his companions harbored a suspicion that Keogh might not be able to locate the grave in question; and with cowboys' fondness for fun, they were not adverse to causing him embarrassment. Keogh was equal to the occasion.

"Now there's a grand suggestion," he seconded. "We'll do this up in style."

Riding watchfully but in silence, Curt took note that they headed in the direction of Hendricks' spread. But his hopes of a close approach were dashed as they crossed an edge of the Folly and worked deeper toward the vast, remote sprawl of the Jackson Ranch. Here was broken, inhospitable country, where, as Tone had warned, it became necessary to leave the buckboard behind and proceed on horseback. Even such locomotion threatened to become difficult if not impossible.

It was easy to see how whole herds might vanish in such a country, leaving no trace. He half expected Mrs. Abernathy to inquire as to the reason for a cemetery so remote from town, but perhaps she guessed the explanation for so lonely a grave.

Keogh halted, indicating a spot where a wooden marker had rotted beyond recognition, and the sod looked almost as unbroken as that which surrounded it. He seemed preoccupied as the rosebush was planted, Jennie Abernathy sifting soil about the roots with her own fingers. Keogh helped with a spade, and at his suggestion, a jug of water had been brought to pour around the roots. The other men, hats in hand, watched but offered no comment.

By the time they returned to town, it was too late for anything else. Mrs. Abernathy was given a room at the Palace, whence she proposed to start back the next day. Keogh, lounging in the lobby while Curt shaved, was hailed as Mrs. Abernathy descended for supper.

"I hope there's a good eating place in this town, Mr. Keogh," she said. "I find the art of cookery almost a lost art in many places which call themselves restaurants."

"I know what you mean," Keogh agreed sympathetically. "However, the restaurant in this town is not so bad as some. Won't you join Curt and myself at supper?"

Professing herself delighted, she produced a magazine and handed it to him while they waited for Curt to appear.

"This advertisement might interest you," she suggested. "It caught my attention before I embarked upon this journey because of what seemed a coincidence. Here blooded stock were being offered for sale from Cactus Valley, which was my destination."

It was a farm and home magazine, published in the East, Keogh saw. The advertisement was for the Jackson Herefords, pedigreed stock now at last being offered for sale, after long years of building up the herd.

Keogh was abstracted as they ate. The coming of the railroad made it possible to sell on a nation-wide basis, rather than to a local market. Under such conditions, thoroughbred cattle would bring at least ten times as much as if sold for meat. Someone with a shrewd business sense must be managing the Jackson Ranch.

He commented on another aspect after returning from supper.

"It would be next to impossible to build up a herd of pure-bred stock on most ranches, without fences, and with open range prevailing. But they just might manage back on Jackson's. You noticed today, I suppose, how remote and isolated it is from everywhere else?"

"I sure did," Curt conceded. "Maybe that's what they're doing back in there—but the thought crossed my mind that missing cattle could get lost back there, too."

"It's a notion that will bear looking into," Keogh admitted. "It'll be a job for us."

Curt sighed. "Do we have to do that before we go

back to talk about that cattle deal at Hendricks'?" he asked wistfully.

Keogh forebore a gentle jibe at his friend's condition. Curt had really been smitten by a pair of bright eyes.

"Maybe we can make a sort of combined social and business call there in the morning," he suggested.

With the morning, however, came an interruption. Along with Zeke, O'Malley and Whipple, they watched Mrs. Abernathy embark upon the return journey. As the dust of the receding stage settled, Whipple replaced his hat and turned accusingly to Keogh.

"So you knew the proper place, and you're a gent of integrity, who wouldn't deceive a trusting old lady?" he chided. " 'And said rose shall bloom above the old coot's grave.' Sounded to the rest of us like a promise. Only, as Zeke and Tom and me more or less recollect, it was on a horse thief's grave we ended up plantin' this memento!"

"Get your horses." Keogh shrugged resignedly. "I figured you'd bring that up. But when it comes to that, wasn't Abernathy a horse thief his own self?"

"Why, now you mention it, there have been rumors to the effect that that was why they hung him," Whipple conceded. "But still and all, that particular horse thief wasn't the one Mrs. Abernathy had in mind."

"He wasn't just the one I had in mind, either, to start with," Keogh admitted. "But there were reasons for turnin' aside, her being such a sweet and trusting lady."

They went with him, still skeptically, and retraced the previous day's route to where the rose stood. It was just coming into blossom, apparently having suffered no setback from the transplanting. After pausing to admire it, they continued, by devious ways, on and around a wide canyon. It had served as a barrier, effectively shutting others away from the grave to which he finally brought them. It seemed to Curt that this was some of the wildest, most inaccessible country he had ever looked upon, and the mysterious Jackson Ranch lay behind the barrier.

Here, unlike the sunken patch of soil where the rosebush now reposed, the land bore a marker, not a rotted remnant of a board. A large native sandstone had been laboriously rolled into place, and on it an inscription had been laboriously chiseled. The carving had been done by an artisan of considerable skill.

If that was surprising, the message was still more so.

"In Loving Memory
of our Husband, George Abernathy,
This memento placed by
Rose Running Horse
and
Carrie Spotted Fawn."

"He gave white names to those women," Keogh explained. "And so naturally they wanted to do things white fashion, even to erecting a marker for him.

When I started recollectin' the facts, there they were.
And that stone's too big to move, and too conspicuous
to hide."

Zeke blew his nose loudly. Whipple studied the
weathered marker.

"In loving memory," he repeated. "I apologize,
Keogh. I reckon the rose was planted over the right
horse thief."

10

Pratt had bided his time with well-concealed impatience, a role in which he had trained himself over a long period. If it had been vexing to lose to Keogh at dice, it had been downright embarrassing to be caught and exposed at attempted robbery, then turned loose as though the matter were too trifling to be pursued. It left Keogh holding the whip hand, a condition which could not long be allowed to continue.

The messenger who had been dispatched to Hendricks returned with an indecisive report. Hendricks had studied over the request for information for several minutes before uneasily making up his mind. But having taken no action after his employee had reported the suspicion attaching to Keogh's horse, he could not afford to admit such a dereliction. Besides, there was Curt, and the possible displeasure of his women-folks should he get Curt and Keogh into trouble.

A second messenger required longer to make the journey and return, but his report was alarming.

"I couldn't find hide nor hair of either of the boys," he confessed, the boys in question being the pair who had sought to ambush the new arrivals. "But I did find a dead horse."

"What sort of a dead horse?" Pratt demanded eagerly.

"Wasn't too much of it left," was the reply. "The coyotes and magpies had been at it—but there was enough sign left to be interestin'."

"Well?" Pratt prodded.

"I couldn't make out whether it'd ever had a brand or not. Not enough hide left. But from what hide there was, it might have been a dead ringer for the cayuse this Keogh is ridin' now."

Such a similarity could mean much, or nothing. "Go on," Pratt growled.

"There was one other thing. This horse's hoofs had been worn down, same as those on the horse Curt is riding. Might be that they shot Keogh's horse; then he got hold of Brick's, which looked plenty like it."

The possibility was disturbing, though not nearly so much so as the disappearance of Brick and his companion. There was enough evidence to justify the conclusion that neither of them would be returning.

"I guess we know enough," Pratt decided. "Cattle buyers, eh? If that's what they are, they can buy their next herds in Boot Hill!"

Whipple, Tone and O'Malley, mollified by the discovery, turned back. Keogh lingered; so Curt did the same as a matter of course. He waited with increasing impatience for Keogh to head toward the XT, now the Double Diamond with an I.

"You still looking for something here?" he asked finally.

"I think perhaps I see how the major's herd did a vanishing act," Keogh suggested. They had partially retraced their steps to a turn made the day before. He pointed.

"Do you see any route there—a trail through the canyon, for instance?"

Curt's head shake was bewildered.

"There's a canyon, all right, but it comes to a dead end, in a solid wall of rock. You seemed sort of surprised to come up against it yesterday."

"I was more than surprised; I was flabbergasted," Keogh admitted. "That canyon wasn't blocked when I last rode through here a few years ago. It was an open pass, maybe twenty feet wide—the only one for quite a way in either direction. Up there," he pointed to the rim of the canyon, "was a boulder about the size of a small house. It gave the appearance of being so precariously perched that a strong wind might topple it—only I suppose it had been balanced there for centuries."

Startled, Curt looked more closely. There was no boulder perched above the rim, but the mass which filled the opening, wall to wall, might well be the same stone the size of a house.

"You mean it's been toppled—pushed over to choke the opening?"

"It would require quite a push; probably a nudge of dynamite served," Keogh replied. "Anybody who didn't know this back country pretty well might not even realize what had happened—especially in or after a heavy snowstorm."

The herd had been run off from the post during such a storm, Curt reflected.

"Let's have a look at the other side," Keogh added.

That required some doing. Leaving their horses, they had to climb sharply to find a way to the top, then to the far side beyond the boulder which choked the passage. Once more in the canyon, Keogh looked expectantly at Curt.

"You good at reading sign, after it's old?" he asked.

There was not much remaining, but enough; a few dry cow chips, even the marks of hoofs, not quite obliterated by time and the elements.

"You think the herd was driven through here?"

"It could have been. Cattle certainly came this way, despite the fact that the canyon's plugged so tight that nothing other than a mountain goat could get through. If that big boulder was nudged so it tumbled, after they'd passed, but before searchers came along —well, it fooled you, and it mighty near fooled me, who'd seen this place before. Take a search party who had never been here, and they could be counted to pass by without even guessing there had once been a trail through. And the herd, held back beyond, could vanish—as they did."

Curt nodded, not quite satisfied.

"That could account for the herd stolen from the Army," he admitted. "But there have been others vanishing since then, and *after* that route was plugged!"

Keogh shook his head in frustration.

"That's what's got me guessing," he confessed. "We've got an answer, but not the answer. And I've a hunch it's tied in with something big, something we won't like!"

Keogh was still mulling the matter over when they arrived at Hendricks', again to a warm greeting. There were too many leads here, as though some of them had been deliberately tossed out to be found; found and followed to a frustrating conclusion, while the real solution remained, perhaps out in the open but invisible nevertheless.

Curt's thoughts were closer to home. He had suspected it before, but now, on further acquaintance, he was sure of it. These people were frightened and uneasy, and not necessarily because of possible suspicion concerning Keogh and himself. Betty, walking beside him, still seemed remote and far removed.

"Something's troubling you," Curt said abruptly. "Can I help?"

Betty stopped, placing her back against the poles of the corral. She looked quickly at him, then away, then back again.

"I don't know," she confessed. "Curt, I'm afraid!" All at once her voice held an urgent appeal.

"Something is wrong in this country, Curt. I don't know what's going on—not really—but something is. I'm sure it involves us—and perhaps you, too. Even Dad is scared. He tries to keep it from Mother and me, but it shows in a lot of ways. And when he is frightened, it's got to be bad. Ordinarily, nothing ever bothers him. I don't know how you and Mr. Keogh are concerned, but I'm sure you are. So I had to speak, to warn you. I wouldn't want you hurt."

It was hard to keep his voice even when he felt like celebrating at this evidence that she might feel as he did, but Curt kept his voice down.

"How do you mean?" he countered. "Why should anybody be bothered by us? We're cattle buyers."

It was the answer he was supposed to give, but it didn't satisfy either of them. This was not acting on Betty's part. He realized that she was not merely afraid, but was asking for help—probably because she didn't know where else to turn.

"Are you really?" she challenged. She colored at the implied doubt, while her eyes searched his. "I'm not questioning your word, Curt—but there are some who don't believe that's what you are—or at least that that's all you're here for. There has been a lot of trouble in this country, and some people say you've been sent here to try to put a stop to it. I'm not saying this very well. Only—if that is so, it could be terribly dangerous. And I'd hate to have you killed!"

"Thanks for telling me. I wouldn't think much of that myself." He managed an uncertain grin. "Folks get some funny notions, don't they?"

"I suppose they do." Not until he and Keogh had taken their departure did she remember that he had offered no denial of the charge. Noting the direction they had gone, she hesitated, then, making a sudden decision, threw a saddle on her own pony. It would do no harm to keep watch for a while, to be sure that her fears were groundless. And if they were not—

Curt was thinking of her warning. He mentioned it as soon as they were safely out of earshot.

"I've a hunch that our period of grace, of poking around as we please, is about used up," he confessed. "Somebody tried to keep us from getting here in the first place—that pair of gunmen wouldn't have been so interested in us on their own account. And that boss man has likely made up his mind as to our business. He's sure that it's not to buy cattle."

"Sounds that way," Keogh conceded. "Let's go call on Jackson. I'm getting more than a little curious about that valley in back of nowhere."

"Speak of the devil." Curt shrugged. "While we were waitin' for dinner just now, I looked over a farm magazine in Hendricks' parlor: the *Stockman's Home Journal*. It's printed in Des Moines. And you know what I found in it? Another ad, about Jackson Herefords."

"Considering the amount of advertising they're doing, they must have a big deal under way."

"Plenty big—and one that appears open and aboveboard. Only one thing strikes me as strange. We haven't had a single report about any of those Herefords ever being rustled. And they'd be worth several times as much as ordinary cattle."

A road from the east led in to Jackson's ranch; it was ordinary except in one respect. For a couple of miles it wound and twisted through a high-walled canyon. At mid-point, which was the border of Jackson's, the way was blocked by a large, inhospitable-looking gate. Most gates were made of poles or barbed wire, but this was built of heavy planks, reinforced with iron bands. It was solid enough to stop bullets, too high for a horse to jump or a man to climb readily. There was no other passage through the canyon.

Its formidable appearance was offset by the fact that the gate stood open, and they rode through without challenge. Off to the south were signs of a creek, creating another barrier to the valley. Stretches of willows and swampy ground were reinforced by an extension of the cliffs from the canyon, stretching low and far. To the south of these was the wasteland of Friedland's Folly. Surveying it, Curt whistled.

"What a place to hold missing herds!" he muttered.

"If you could get them in or out," Keogh concurred. "But this road is said to be the only one, and a herd using it would leave a plain trail."

The canyon widened a mile beyond the gate, and there were a barn, bunk house and corral. Loungers near the barn watched their approach with apparent indifference. Keogh's request to see the boss met with a counter-question.

"You fellows the cattle buyers we've heard about?"

"That's our business," Keogh granted.

"Then you're wastin' your time. You're welcome to look around, if you like, but we don't sell any animals for beef. If that's what you want, you wouldn't be able to come within shoutin' distance of the prices we get."

"Maybe not, but I'd like to talk with Mr. Jackson," Keogh persisted. "Any reason why not?"

"None a-tall, exceptin' he's back East right now, looking after business matters."

It required a swing of miles, back to Friedland's Folly instead of toward the town, but it was clear to Curt that Keogh was in no mood for further balks. If the open front door showed nothing, they would try the closed one at the back.

Betty Hendricks sighed with relief when they turned back, but she watched with apprehension as they changed course and headed for the Folly. Like herself, they clearly suspected that there was some secret here—one which might better remain undiscovered. But her own curiosity equalled their own, and again she followed reluctantly, though well behind and out of sight.

11.

Keogh did not take the more obvious route toward the old warehouse. Instead he led the way deeper toward the jungle-like growth where the creek which marked the border between Jackson's and the Folly turned and twisted, a long barrier against further progress toward the big valley.

Trees and a tangle of lush undergrowth made for difficult going under the best of conditions. Impenetrable thickets blocked the way, and mosquitoes were a torment. This was wilderness, the country of bobcat and beaver, coyote and catamount, but certainly not of cattle. Finally, as both had expected, they found a trail.

It was more like a road, long unused. Here and there were the half-washed out marks of hoofs, proof that it had been traveled by cattle. Where no natural route could be found, trees had been cut and dragged out of sight. But care had been taken to leave as little sign of this as possible.

"They've been sawed off close to the ground, not

cut with an axe," Keogh pointed out. "And notice how dirt and gravel have been hauled in and spread to cover the stumps, to cover the sign showing it's a road."

"You think this is where the missing herds have been moved?" Curt asked. "On to the Jackson Ranch, then held there? You think that talk of pure-breds was just a cover-up?"

Keogh shook his head in disagreement. "I've a notion that this is something bigger than mere rustling. Those cattle we saw there are Herefords, and they look like blooded stock."

"If they are, ordinary cattle would be a nuisance, especially longhorns. Still, the valley's probably big enough for several fields. O'Malley said something about hating to be a barbed-wire cowboy."

"And he used to work for Cole Jackson," Keogh agreed. "Likewise, why should Jackson run advertisements in farm papers in all parts of the country unless he had something to sell?"

"That's your question. And right about now, we should be getting back to town. When we don't show up on schedule—you think somebody will maybe start looking for us?"

"I'd hate to bet on their not doing it," Keogh admitted.

The trail had clearly been unused for months, perhaps since the previous summer. It led straight toward Jackson's. Where the ground was soft, hoofs had beaten a deep trail. Only big herds could have caused that.

"Set a Judas steer to lead, and a herd would follow without much trouble," Keogh observed. "Once on this road, it's the only route they could take."

"Yeah," Curt agreed. "But take to where? Would they maybe sprout wings—or fins—when they got this far?"

All at once the creek was ahead, and the trail terminated abruptly at its bank. The stream, as far as they could see in either direction, was sluggish but very deep. In addition, it was as wide as a river. Cattle would be forced to swim. Following a leader, they could perhaps be induced to take to the water, despite its forbidding appearance. It would be impossible to go to either side along the creek banks.

The stumper here was the opposite shore, a frowning barrier. The continuing line of cliffs reared up at the water's edge. The wall was not high, some five to eight feet, but it was unbroken. Horses or cattle, swimming, would be unable to scramble over.

No breaks which would afford a crossing were visible in the wall in either direction. Yet the road led directly to this dead end, and unquestionably it had been used.

Their horses snorted distrustfully, disliking the look of the black water, not wanting to set foot in it. A plunge would engulf them. Curt found a long pole and thrust it down. Though a dozen feet in length, it did not touch bottom.

"Somebody's crazy," he pronounced. "Whether it's us or not, I'd hate to say. But from what I know about cattle, they wouldn't set foot in that water, no matter how hard they were shoved and pushed from behind. And if they did get out there, they'd mill and drown. What else *could* they do?"

Their horses, ground-hitched, were feeding hungrily on the grass which had grown up in the unused roadway. Aside from the mosquitoes, the place seemed lifeless, so remote that neither bird nor animal revealed itself; no fish jumped from the black water.

This was the edge of the Folly, and the Folly was supposed to be haunted. Curt could well believe it. He turned, then stared in amazement. Keogh was a dozen feet out from the shore, and he appeared to be walking on the water.

Catching the look on his friend's face, Keogh grinned.

"Come on out," he suggested. "The water's fine. Nothing to it."

He returned to shore, splashing shallowly, and Curt now made out what Keogh's ever ready curiosity had discovered. Perhaps half a foot beneath the water, virtually invisible in so dark a stream unless one looked carefully, was a bridge. But it was a bridge under, not over the water.

Uneasily, he followed Keogh's lead, stepping out, finding the planks beneath his feet solid enough, examining the planks at either end. The bridge—if such a term was applicable under the circumstances—seemed to be perhaps fifteen feet wide. It headed straight across to the opposite side, and they walked across, to be halted again by the barrier of the cliff, some seven feet high at that point.

"Give me a boost," Keogh requested, and was on the top of the wall. He disappeared on the far side. A minute passed. Then, not much to Curt's surprise, for he had begun to suspect the answer, the apparently solid wall began to move.

The wall, not much more than a foot in thickness, was opening. A section as wide as the bridge swung slowly, the opening leaving a passage-way on either side. Keogh was shoving against the end of the opening gate.

"Somebody's done a lot of work here, gone to a lot of trouble. And it was probably worth it," he pointed out, stepping back. Once he quit pushing, the slab of stone swung of its own balance back into place, closing the gap as though it had never existed.

"That stone is quite soft—you can cut it with a knife." He demonstrated. "Likely the softness gave somebody the notion in the first place. It has been sawed through at each end and underneath, the cuts at the ends made at an angle. Then it was jacked up and set on a pivot. It wouldn't be very hard to do, with the proper tools."

The rimrock here was a remnant of the canyon

which guarded the main entrance to Jackson's Ranch and the valley it occupied.

"Push it open here, and the barrier is out of the way," Keogh explained. "Then shut the gate, and unless someone knew of it, nobody would ever guess at anything of the sort."

"It fooled me," Curt conceded. "And this explains part of the deal. But I still can't understand how they could get a herd to cross. If some were forced onto the bridge, they'd still be terrified and mill around and plunge off on both sides. Of course," he added thoughtfully, "ropes might be strung from both shores. But I still don't see how you'd induce cattle to walk out there, even if they had a leader."

"I don't understand, either," Keogh agreed. "But those fellows are smart, and they managed. They made use of some of the lumber from the old warehouse to build the bridge. No one would know, or get suspicious, on seeing several loads of planks hauled in."

Part of the wall of the warehouse had been torn away. It fitted. Building the bridge could have been done as secretly as the construction of the road, and, save in one respect, without much difficulty.

"I'd think it would be mighty hard to work under water, even a few inches under," Curt objected.

"My guess is that it would be next to impossible," Keogh conceded. "Let's do some more looking around. This is getting interesting."

They returned to the south shore, then set out downstream on foot. It would have been impossible to tell which was downstream had they not seen the creek at another point. It was a chore to push through matted brush and undergrowth, but their reward came a quarter of a mile downstream. There, around a bend and safely out of sight of the road or bridge, the creek narrowed to less than half of its former width. Here, too, were more high, rocky banks on either side.

It was a perfect spot for a dam, and a dam had been built, someone again making use of some of the planks from the old warehouse on the Folly. Moss grew along the line of the dam, where the water spilled over in a smooth light sheet, a drop of half a dozen feet to the stream below. There were gates in the dam, now closed, which could be opened with a pull of a lever.

Now the answer was simple enough. The dam had been built after the bridge was installed. When the gates were closed, the water was backed up, covering the bridge and all traces of a road. But once the sluice gates were opened, it would require only a few hours to lower the stream level to a point where the bridge again would be above the water.

After a herd had been moved across, the bridge would be submerged. Manifestly, the scheme had worked well. Few people ever ventured into such a remote wilderness, even under normal conditions. On one side, the one nearer the Jackson Ranch, were brush and swamp, and it could be guarded against intrusion. On the south side, the fearsome reputation of Friedland's Folly had kept intruders away.

Also, on the southern limits of the road was Hendricks' spread. It all added up to an unpleasant but inescapable conclusion. Both outfits must be engaged in nefarious operations, working together.

Observing Curt's long face, Keogh had no trouble reading his thoughts.

"Don't take it too hard," he advised. "I'm sure that Betty and Mrs. Hendricks don't have any real notion what Hendricks is up to—and I'd even go so far as to suspect that he doesn't know about half of this himself. My hunch is that he's just an employee, not the boss, and is being used as a front."

"But he's got to know of this," Curt said stubbornly.

"I suppose so. But have you noticed one curious thing? We've heard a lot of stories about rustlers and missing herds—but there have been no reports of any missing herd since last fall! I've a strong suspicion that maybe the rustling served a double purpose, the first of which was to bring in a good income until something bigger was ready to come off the fire."

"And now it's coming to a boil?"

"What do *you* think?"

Curt scratched a cheek, not entirely because of the ministrations of a mosquito.

"Could be. But what could be bigger than rustling

on such a scale."

"That," Keogh returned grimly, "is what we're going to find out!"

"What was the second reason you mentioned?"

"The rustling—with attention centered on Hendricks and his spread—would draw attention away from Jackson's. What could do that better than a herd that had obviously been stolen after being sold—and to the Army, no less—then brought back with a brand not too much altered? That strikes me as a touch of pure genius."

"And the real center of trouble is up in Jackson's valley?"

"That's where this road and bridge seem to point."

"So we go back there again—only this time in by the back door?"

"I doubt if we'll ever have a better chance."

"Or even a second one, if we don't take this," Curt agreed.

Leading their horses, not without difficulty, they got them across the concealed bridge. Once satisfied that there was solid footing, the horses crossed, still snorting distrustfully. They seemed as surprised as Curt at having a way opened in the rock wall, and relieved at finding solid ground on the far side.

By this time the sun was sinking out of sight, which fitted in nicely with their plans. It would hardly do to prowl the valley by day, but if they could have the night in which to look around, they might well unearth whatever secrets it concealed.

The swampy land and heavy growth of willows was soon left behind. Mountains loomed to the north, another natural barrier. Between was a big country, an impressive valley. Here, to the west of the gate, was a land known to few.

The last rays of the sun seemed to focus on a spiderweb pattern, which could be nothing other than a wide-reaching fence of several strands of barbed wire. In this valley, rustled herds could have been held, with no one the wiser.

Keogh surveyed the land, his face grim. There were two roads in or out from the valley: the one guarded by the big gate, which could be quickly closed; the other the secret bridge by which they had come. He snapped his fingers in a sudden gesture of disgust.

"What now?" Curt asked.

"I'm crazy," Keogh said plaintively. "Why didn't we ask Whipple and Tone and O'Malley what this Jackson Ranch was like? They used to work here."

"Used to," Curt repeated significantly. "Not any more."

"Those three boys are reasonably honest, same as you or me. So there's some things they wouldn't go for. Apparently they don't really suspect the truth of what has been going on back in here."

"Still, things reached a point where they might have gotten the wind up. So they were given their time."

"Did you ever take note of one thing?" Keogh asked. "It just now struck me. Those boys are scared. Maybe they don't know what's going on, and likely they don't want to—but I have a hunch that they're suspicious that maybe they know too much. They didn't even want to talk to me about anything beyond the ordinary."

"Now you mention it, it does sort of stack up that way. Only—"

"Something on your mind?"

"Just that they're still sticking around."

"Could be like a man with a bull by the tail." Keogh frowned. "Scared to hang on, but twice as scared to let go."

"You know, I'm getting that sort of feeling myself," Curt returned, and this time he did not smile.

The valley, as they obtained increasingly better views, was impressive. There were creeks, smaller hills, and wide stretches of timbered land, interspersed with vast open meadows. Ahead, for the first time, save at a distance, they saw some of the blooded stock for which the ranch was famous.

Here and there, while making their long ride from the Nebraska country, they had come upon cattle which approached these for quality, usually small herds. Quality beef were rare. These, unmistakably, were quality.

They were sleek and well fed, red animals with

white faces and horns less than half the size of most.

"They look as good as those advertisements make them out to be," Curt conceded.

"They sure do," Keogh agreed. "And this has been a good place to build up such a herd, away from others which might cross with them and spoil the strain. The barbed-wire has taken care of rustled herds. I heard of this ranch when I was in this country before. Jackson was just getting a start then. I never saw his ranch, never dreamed there was such a big valley back in here. I don't believe that most people, even old settlers, have any notion what's it's like."

"It's big, all right." Curt rubbed his stomach wistfully. "Too bad we didn't bring along some grub. I'm getting sharp-set again."

"There's a house off there." Keogh pointed it out. "See that trace of smoke above the trees?"

The cabin was among big trees, nearly concealed in a coulee's mouth. Though miles from the regular ranch buildings, it apparently was occupied.

"Must be a line cabin," Curt observed. "You think we dare risk askin' for a meal?"

"Not openly. But there is such a thing as uninvited guests. In other words, we'll—"

The crash of a gun, smashing against the silence, came jarringly against their eardrums.

12.

To move for cover was instinctive, but this time it was clear that they were not the intended target. A moment later it was apparent that the shot had not actually been fired at anyone, but into the air, by way of a warning.

Keogh glimpsed a furtive figure, who had been skulking along a path, leaving it for the denser cover of trees and a scattering of brush. It looked as though he had been stealing away from the cabin. He halted, then turned as the gunman appeared at the corner of the house, weapon pointed skyward. His attitude was negligent but reproving.

"Now, now, Professor," he chided, "you know better'n to try that. Ain't one time enough? Besides, it's risky. Last time you had on them whiskers, and this time I do believe you've got on Chin Loo's overcoat. I might be fooled into mistakin' you for somebody you ain't, and shoot where I oughtn't to. And anyhow, you know matters are too important right now for you to get drunk again."

The fugitive hesitated, then turned back resignedly. His voice was complaining.

"You are like all your kind, too trigger-happy.

How do you expect me to think, to work, under such conditions of strain? *Mein Gott*, but cannot a man take even a walk for a bit of exercise? You think maybe I can stand it, to be cooped up like the chickens be?"

The gunman was a slight figure, especially by comparison with the solid bulk of the Professor. He spun the revolver by the trigger guard, on one finger.

"First time I ever knew you to take any interest in exercise, beyond liftin' food or drink to your face. Anyhow, after the way you snuck off to town, there's no use givin' me that line. You finish up the job, and after that you can drink a saloon dry, for all I care. "Why," he added disapprovingly, "it's taken you all this time to sober up, after what you guzzled in town."

"What I had was but a taste," the Professor snorted. "It was like a summer shower to the desert. My system requires more. It craves the whiskey, which alone can lubricate the wheels of the mind. Never have I gone so long without it. This way, I cannot work, for I cannot think."

"You're doing fine, and you'll keep right on with the job," the guard warned grimly. "Only don't go getting notions about how valuable that carcass of yours is. Things are far enough along now; we could manage without you. You try runnin' out on us, and the boss said to put a bullet in you."

"He would kill me—me, the only one who can

do what he would have done?" The Professor was outraged. "The man is a fool. You are a fool. All those about me are fools. And I am the greatest of all, to work for so stupid a bunch."

"Yeah, yeah, I reckon we're all fools together. But those cattle cars have arrived, which means it's up to you to do your job—and do it right, if you want your pay *and* whiskey in just a couple of days now. So let's get started."

He gestured with the gun, less playfully; then the door slammed behind them. Curt nudged Keogh.

"The Professor's the fellow who was loose in town the other night, wearing those false whiskers that came off in my hand."

Keogh nodded. Apparently the Professor had not gotten far after slipping out of the saloon.

"They've got him doing some job back in here, and he tries to kick over the traces," Curt went on. "A big brain, maybe, but not smart enough for the native cunning of an old ranny like that."

Some men could go for long periods without a taste of alcohol, but then the craving would come upon them, an almost irresistible desire. Only a prolonged spree would satisfy them.

Such a craving was upon the Professor now, and liquor was being denied him because he had work to do, some task which might suffer from a delay of several days. Refused the whiskey he craved, he had disguised himself and escaped to town to obtain a few drinks. The drinks had whetted his appetite without satisfying it. Now he was driven by raging desire.

A distraction came as a window slid up with a rasping sound, only to hesitate and plop back in place. It was raised anew, a shrill voice chattering a complaint, and this time it was propped open with a stick. The voice was that of the cook, Chin Loo. When the window was secured, a pie, so hot from the oven that the steam still rose, was placed on the sill to cool.

"Now that's what I call a kindly act," Curt whispered, eying the pie. "It looks as if they feed the Professor well, even if they don't let him have his toddy. But since he's so ungrateful—"

He sidled to the window, then returned with the pie to where Keogh waited.

"Smells like sarvis berry," Curt murmured. "Look at those purple juices!"

The pie proved as tasty as it looked. Curt sighed comfortably as he wiped his mouth.

"I feel berry much better, as you might say," he observed. "What next?"

A sudden jabbering, filled with anger and anguish, testified to the fact that Chin Loo had returned to take the pie in. A moment later the worried voice of the guard chimed in.

"Too bad he couldn't have been patient a couple of minutes longer," Curt observed philosophically. "I was fixing to leave the empty plate on the ground near the window, upside down. Then he could guess what had done it."

As it was, the guard was obviously jumping to the logical conclusion: that the pie had been stolen; not merely swiped. The difference was a difference between a local hand, hungry and tempted, and intruders like themselves. No open alarm was sounded, but a hunt might already be under way.

The closing night was in their favor. They moved on foot to where corrals loomed like spidery threads against the horizon, the uneasy bawling of cattle indicating that they were occupied. Unlike the average outfit, this one had not two or three corrals, but at least a dozen in a series, most of them crowded with cattle.

"Must be getting them ready for shipment," Curt suggested. "This looks like a big operation."

"One where the patient dies?" Keogh returned, half in irony, then pondered his own words. These cattle were thoroughbreds, worth far more than the ordinary run, therefore deserving of better care. It was reasonable to assume that the Professor, as he had been dubbed, was a veterinarian, perhaps an expert on the diseases of cattle.

Even as they watched, and despite the poor light, they saw several men at work in one of the corrals shoving the cattle, one at a time, through a chute. Each was held long enough for a flurry of struggle, as though some operation were being performed.

"Inoculating them for blackleg, perhaps," Keogh suggested, "or maybe something else, before they're shipped out around the country."

"Doesn't hurt them much, apparently," Curt observed. "But it don't just please them, either. This is really a big operation."

"Whatever it is, the Professor supplies the know-how, but the hands do the work," Keogh added. "He's not helping there. Looks like another cabin, way off there at the side. Let's have a look."

A single light shone, like a low-hung star. This cabin was about a mile from the one where the Professor was kept as an unwilling tenant, hills hiding one from the other. The large number of houses on the ranch was another curious and unusual factor.

"One thing's got me guessing," Curt confessed. "With an outfit like this, why would Jackson dabble in rustling and maybe murder on the side? Of, course, it's a mighty big operation, and maybe he needs some revenue till he starts selling the Herefords."

"Not much doubt about that part," Keogh agreed. "But I'd make you a good-sized bet that Jackson's not running this, any more than Hendricks runs his ranch. Hendricks is a front for someone else—and Jackson could be, too."

"If it's neither of them, who's got the brain and ability to plan and head up a deal like this?"

"That," Keogh returned grimly, "is what we're going to find out."

A man worked busily at a desk in the single lighted room of the house, the window with its shade but partly drawn. The boldness of the operation, back in that remote valley, indicated that no outside interference was feared. Suspicion had been cleverly diverted to Hendricks' ranch, away from this one, which was clearly the headquarters. Natural barriers and elaborate safeguards gave added protection.

"I'd like to have a look at what he's doing, after he goes to bed," Keogh decided. "Things are getting really interesting—"

He checked as a sudden hubbub erupted on the night, from not far away. The moon had risen, giving a reasonable light, and in it a rider spurred across an open meadow, hotly pursued by several others, who were shouting as they rode. Their alarm was answered by other men who burst out from the screen of trees at the opposite edge of the open space, cutting off the fugitive's retreat.

The rider was caught and dragged from his horse. A wail of distress rent the air, and the cry sounded somehow familiar.

Curt had watched tensely. At the cry he stared in disbelief, then dashed to the rescue, while Keogh watched in dismay. He could hardly blame Curt for responding, for it was Betty Hendricks who had shouted despairingly, and Curt was a man in love. In that instant, nothing else mattered, even that he might be rushing headlong into a trap.

13.

"So this time you found them?"

"Yeah—this time we found them."

The speaker blinked and swallowed uncomfortably under Pratt's heavy stare, not certain what his reaction might be. He blurted out the story in a rush of words.

"They'd been buried way off below the rimrocks—dirt caved down on them. It took a lot of searching, but there they were."

"All right." Pratt's voice was even. "Now we know."

He gave no second thought to the dead men. They deserved what had befallen them. Set to watch and wait, to lie in ambush and kill while themselves unseen—the pair had failed. If they had allowed themselves to be killed instead, it was no great loss.

No real damage had been done. He'd been suspicious of these two who passed themselves off as cattle buyers, and while they undoubtedly had learned a few things from their snooping, they had been unable to act. As representatives of the law, they had to have evidence. He suffered from no such handicap.

They had ridden out to Hendricks' today. Pratt made it his business to know the whereabouts of suspicious characters, to follow each move they made. Hendricks wouldn't like it when something happened to them, but Hendricks didn't count. All that counted was his vengeance!

Vengeance! Pratt rolled the word on his tongue, savoring it like old wine. It had been long in coming, but he had been building toward it for a long, long while. Now the time was at hand.

He scowled, becoming aware that the messenger was staring at his right wrist, at the scar revealed where the sleeve had fallen back. Teslow quailed at the look, then was relieved as Pratt smiled—a twisted, ferocious grin which resembled the leer of a gorilla. Deliberately, he flung back both sleeves, disclosing what had been kept carefully hidden. All at once, with triumph almost within reach, he had to talk, to release some of the bottled-up venom within him.

"Pretty, ain't they?" he asked, viewing the scars. "They're something that lasts—something you don't forget, even if you'd like to. And I've got a matching pair on my ankles. Irons, they call them in the pen— shackles. It takes a long time spent wearin' leg and wrist irons to get such scars."

Teslow swallowed uncertainly. "It must have," he conceded.

"Years," Pratt informed him with a touch of pride. "Days stretchin' like eternity, and each one agony. But I'm getting paid back, with interest, for every ache I suffered! You want to hear the story? Help yourself to a chair."

Teslow licked his lips and sank obediently into a chair. When the boss wanted to talk, it was time to listen.

"I've been thirstin' for vengeance ever since I was a kid," Pratt went on; "since they hanged my Pa, who was as good a man with a long rope or a gun as you'd ever want to see. I was just a kid, but I told the judge that sentenced him that some day I'd make him suffer the same way!"

His eyes were glaring wildly at the remembrance. "He laughed at me—told me to run along and get some sense in my head! I guess part of that was good advice. I got enough sense to keep my mouth shut, till I caught him riding alone. That was half a dozen years later, and I got a rope over a tree limb and the noose around his neck. Then I slashed his horse with my quirt, jumpin' it out from under him, leaving him swingin'!"

His eyes were baleful, clouding as the story unfolded.

"The jerk ought to've broken his neck, he would have, in another minute. But just then, half a dozen riders from one of the ranches come on us sudden. They'd been havin' a night in town, and they took me plumb by surprise. Not that I did too bad. I killed a couple and wounded as many more. But they put seven bullets in me, and the worst part was that they cut down the judge while he was still alive.

"They figured I'd kick off, but I didn't. And later, the judge got back at me, sentencin' me to life at hard labor. To hang and have it over with wouldn't have been so bad, so he wouldn't do that. To go in irons, draggin' a ball and chain—"

Pratt broke off, eying the scars on his wrists, drawing a long, sighing breath. When he went on, his voice was quieter.

"Like I said, those years were worse than dyin'. To start with, I'd only hated the judge. But I changed. I hated everybody—the government, the law, all mankind. I made a new vow, that I'd get out, and the next time I wouldn't make any mistakes. I'd take plenty of time to plan everything, and I'd have a real vengeance—something big and fitting!"

Teslow was impressed. This was a side of the Boss that was rarely revealed. "And you're getting it, rustlin' in a big way!" he guessed.

Pratt laughed disdainfully.

"Rustling? Bah! That's just a cover-up for something bigger, to pay the bills and distract attention from what I'm really doing. I wanted something that everybody would hear about, something to set the whole country talking. I aim to make people—everybody—hate me the way I hate them!"

Teslow was impressed, also somewhat frightened. He covered his uneasiness with the rejoinder:

"That's a pretty big order!"

"You're darned right it is, but you're looking at a man big enough to do the job! It took me quite a while to hit on the right idea. I had to look around for the right place, for a lot of things that would all dovetail together. But I had a piece of luck while I was still in the pen. A lot of news gets back there and gets spread around. All that a man has to do is keep his ears open."

Teslow's answer was revealing. "Yeah, I know how that works."

"You too, eh? Well, one of the crew that had helped put me where I was had come up here to this country and gotten himself a big spread. I don't know just how he managed, and that part didn't matter. I found out all about him and what he was doing here, and when I got the chance, I came and had a look, and I saw right off that it could be worked. So I sort of took over."

"You mean—your saloon here?"

"That was just a starter. Cole Jackson was the man I was after, and he had a big valley and his ranch stocked with thoroughbred Herefords. And the railroad was on the way! Likewise, there was another guy in stir who had the know-how to work things out, given time enough and a chance to experiment. So I brought the Professor along with me."

"He's kind of a nut, ain't he?"

"If you mean that he hates everybody—why, that way he's like me. Those years in the pen had changed me so that Cole Jackson didn't even know me when I saw him. I even worked for him a while, to get the low-down on everything. And now—well, you keep your eyes open and you'll see something bigger'n you ever even dreamed of!"

Teslow's curiosity had been thoroughly whetted, but Pratt seemed to lose interest. An interruption served as a further distraction, as a rider pulled up outside and hurried in by a side door.

"Keogh and his side-kick visited Jackson's today," he explained. "Went in there to snoop, the way it looked."

"And they rode out again without finding anything," Pratt retorted impatiently. "I know all about that."

"Yeah. And after that, they headed for the Folly and up through that brushy country. We lost them in there."

Pratt half rose from the chair. "You lost them—"

The speaker raised a hand, as if to ward off a blow.

"We saw something else, though. Hendricks' girl was watching them, following them, like she was afraid they'd maybe get into trouble. We watched her —and she crossed that bridge, leading her horse!"

Pratt drew a deep breath, then expelled it in a gust of satisfaction.

"That means they're in the valley—which couldn't be better. You know what to do. Only don't kill them. I want them alive."

14.

Curt's rush carried him into the open, almost to the side of the girl, before he sensed that something was wrong. He'd counted on surprise as a big factor in his own favor, hoping to effect a rescue before the others should guess that he was anywhere in the valley.

Instead, the horsemen who pursued Betty were swinging swiftly to deal with him, as though they had expected such a move. Worse, there were twice as many as he'd thought, extra men emerging from the shadows, taking on substance.

So far, no one was shooting. Curt clutched at his own gun, but before he could bring it into action, a pair of lariats, cast from opposite directions, whistled at him. He managed to avoid one loop, flinging up an arm to fend it off, but the other caught him and closed with a jerk, pinning his arms to his sides.

A couple of the crew were subduing Betty, despite her furious struggles. Seeing this, Curt resisted desperately, momentarily expecting Keogh to come to his aid. Then he realized that Keogh wasn't going to do anything so rash, and he was thankful for that as he was borne to the ground, then jerked back to his feet. As long as Keogh remained free, there was hope.

"Where is he?" one man demanded. "Talk fast."

"Where's who?" Curt asked innocently. "What do you mean?"

For answer, a fist smashed his mouth, sending him reeling, drawing a sharp cry from Betty. Held fast by a man on either side, she could do nothing more. The man who towered over him doubled his fist again.

"Don't try to play dumb! I mean Keogh."

"Oh, him?" Curt shook his head, trying to think of a convincing reply, and finding none. "By now he's likely back in town."

A second smash to his mouth drew blood, sprawling him on his back. The crew gathered about were suddenly like a pack of wolves at the scent of blood.

Betty was struggling again, crying out in protest, to no avail. To Keogh, watching tensely from a blacker patch of shadows, it was clear that this had been planned in advance. Somehow they had found out that he and Curt were there, perhaps by following Betty, figuring that she might lead them to the spies. When Curt had responded to her cry of distress, they had been ready.

Now they were deliberately savage. Certain that he was also in the vicinity, they intended to force his hand in much the same manner. If he remained silent and refused to rise to the bait, it would be almost impossible to find him, at least while the night lasted. And a man prowling the valley might learn a lot during those hours of darkness.

Not all of the brutality was simulated. A man who would send out bushwhackers, with orders to kill on sight, would surround himself with others of like mind. This crew was calloused by long years of outlawry, eager to vent their hate on anyone who worked for the law.

Exactly how far they would go against Curt, Keogh was not certain, but it was quickly apparent that they could not stop far short of maiming and crippling. They must be convinced that he was watching, so Curt was the key to force him to reveal himself.

That might mean death for both of them in the end, with his own coming in equally unpleasant fashion. But Curt was his partner, and he had to do something.

A shot, whether aimed to frighten or to kill, would serve as a distraction, but if it attracted attention to himself, without really serving them, it would be worse than useless. The other alternative seemed to be to get the drop on them, which he might do possibly long enough to free Curt and Betty from their clutches.

But since the valley was swarming with enemies and no escape from it was in sight, freedom for all three of them might be of very brief duration. They were gathered under a fairly tall, large evergreen, a jack pine by its look. There was no wind, but the upper branches swayed violently. Keogh looked closer.

Apparently Curt was not the only one who had been taken by surprise. Someone or something had frightened into taking to the branches of the tree, a somewhat insecure perch apparently. It was too dark to be certain, but Keogh guessed that it might be either a bobcat or a bear cub; more likely the latter. A cat would be more at home on such a perch, less nervous.

Not that it greatly mattered. If he could both attract and distract its attention, and in doing so disconcert the group under the tree—

Inspiration came suddenly. There were no stones nearby for throwing, but he had something better, a handful of the heavy iron washers which he'd found at the old packing house, and which had already proved useful. Keogh clutched them, then threw a fistful, aiming for the dark huddle in the upper reaches of the tree.

An iron washer could prove a vicious missile, and the handful, whizzing and striking like a swarm of hornets, had their effect. The thing in the tree had been clinging, motionless but with an unhappy sense of insecurity. Now it emitted an anguished howl, lost its hold and half-fell, half-slid, grabbing for a hold without obtaining one. The thoroughly frightened cub plopped among the equally startled crew, then took off for taller timber at accelerated speed.

Any confusion in the mind of the cub was duplicated among the crew. The distraction had been complete, though not enough to allow Curt or Betty to escape. Heated discussion, mixed with recriminations, followed. It was Teslow who came up with something in one hand and a pertinent observation concerning it.

"Somebody threw something and hit the cub," he pointed out. "Must have been a bunch of these old iron washers. If I was makin' a gues, which I am, I'd say it was most likely Keogh that did it."

That had its sobering effect, as Keogh had hoped. He was somewhere about, and all the rest of them knew as much concerning his whereabouts as did the prisoners. To question them further would be not only useless but very possibly dangerous. For Keogh undoubtedly had a gun.

They hustled the prisoners away, the extra crewmen spreading out, silent now and twice as dangerous as before. The valley would soon be swarming with men on the hunt. For the present, it was out of the question even to think about a rescue.

An exclamation, quickly suppressed, told him that some of the searchers had come upon his own and Curt's horses. Now he was really afoot, but the loss did not worry him greatly. Escape from the well-guarded valley would be difficult under any circumstances, but doubly so on horseback.

In any case, he wasn't ready to leave.

Events were fast approaching a climax. A time-table had been set up, based on the completion of the railroad. Now that it was operating, nothing could be allowed to interfere. Quite clearly, they did not consider him as much of a threat. Since he couldn't escape, they'd hunt him down, later if not sooner.

Such an appraisal might be realistic, however discouraging. Keogh shrugged it aside. As in a game of cards, you played and waited for the breaks, and there was generally some luck for those who were ready to take advantage of it. If he failed when it came, the miscalculation could prove fatal.

The night was alive with ghostly movement. Many men were riding, criss-crossing the general vicinity, almost deliberately drawing attention to themselves. While they did that, others on foot prowled with the eager ruthlessness of minks or weasels. The search was widening, but they were confident that he could not escape from the valley. Even if he should get back to the creek and try to swim, keen-eyed watchers would pick him off with rifles.

Motionless, then moving as conditions required, Keogh waited until the night calmed. The twittering of a bird, the rustle of small rodents, confirmed his judgment that the hunt had shifted. They were prob-aby expecting him to put as much distance as pos-sible between the place where he had been and the point he would find himself on the arrival of a new day.

In the cabin where the man had been at work, the light had gone out. Undoubtedly the fellow had joined in the hunt. Keogh had a strong curiosity about what the desk might contain.

The door was unlocked, and he let himself in. Enough moonlight penetrated to enable him to move about with reasonable ease. The house was empty.

This was much more than a line cabin; it had four good rooms. At the least, it must belong to a foreman. Keogh returned to the desk, its roll-top closed but not locked. Inside, the cubbyholes were stuffed with envelopes. The postmarks were nearly all different, from widely separated sections of the country. Selecting a few at random, Keogh moved to where the light was good enough for reading.

Some were preliminary correspondence, but there were many orders for cattle, to be shipped when the railroad was equipped to handle business. Many orders were for only a few head, for cows or a bull, while some buyers wanted several. It was clear that advertisements in the various farm publications had gotten good results.

The records for the entire transaction were in the desk, from initial inquiries to orders, with money orders or bank drafts enclosed in payment, according to stated terms: one half down, the balance to be paid on delivery.

None of the money was there. Apparently the drafts had been cashed as soon as they were received. At the prices, a handsome profit had already been realized.

Keogh observed that, while the name of Cole Jackson was occasionally mentioned, all business was done in the name of the foreman, H. P. Shelhammer. That was interesting, since the foreman's name was Smith—or had been, according to the latest knowledge of Tone, Whipple and O'Malley, who had once worked on the ranch.

A full train of cattle would be loaded out soon, and shipped east to a distribution point. At St. Paul or Omaha it would be divided up, some cars continuing on east, other going southeast or southwest. The animals in these would in turn be shipped to particular buyers.

A separate stack of envelopes, addressed and ready for mailing, except for sealing, contained the names and pedigree of each animal. Everything was in proper order.

Outwardly, there was nothing wrong, nothing that would excite suspicion. The whole transaction appeared to be aboveboard and legitimate. Yet everything pointed to some giant swindle, or worse. Men did not rustle whole herds, or build concealed bridges, or take other elaborate precautions, including hiring a crew who hunted intruders as ruthlessly as wolves, where honesty prevailed.

All this was interesting, but not particularly surprising. Keogh closed the desk, then, remembering his real mission, searched anew. It took a while to find what he was after, but his hunch that whiskey would be kept about the premises proved sound. There were half a dozen quart bottles in a wooden box in one corner, concealed under a pile of old clothing.

Keogh took a bottle, noting the brand name: Willow Run, 86 proof. It was the same as that sold in Pratt's saloon in Cactus Valley. Nowhere else in that part of the country had Keogh found this brand.

The Professor, he was sure, would be pleased with such a gift.

The house where the Professor was held a virtual prisoner was dark.

Apparently there were no dogs in the valleys, which was a piece of luck. Dogs might worry the cattle, who were too valuable to be harried.

A small, lean-to-type of room had been built off from the kitchen, apparently to serve as sleeping quarters for the cook. The window was open, which was strange, since most foreigners believed the night air to be populated by demons. A faint perfume emanated from the window, battling a stronger, less pleasant odor which seemed to permeate the air about this house.

Keogh sniffed, striving to sort out the divergent smells. The stronger, with which the house must have become saturated over a long period, was reminiscent of a chemistry laboratory. That which drifted from the lean-to room was of another character entirely—the sweetish scent of opium. Apparently, with his day's work out of the way, the cook had indulged himself in a pipe.

The Professor would not be allowed to join in the manhunt, so the guard must be somewhere in the vicinity. Keogh discovered him, seated at the front of the house, his straight-backed chair tipped back against the closed door. A six-shooter, lying in his lap, caught the faint reflection of the high-riding moon. His mustache, rivaling that of a walrus, rose and fell gently with his snoring.

It was unlikely that the cook's room, built as an afterthought, had any connection with the rest of the house. The other windows were tightly closed. Each one, aside from that of the cook, was set with heavy iron bars. Whatever the task for which the Professor was employed, he was not trusted.

A few nights ago, by disguising himself, he'd succeeded in getting away and into town, and obtaining a few drinks before being caught. Now he was safely back. No doubt, recognizing his own limitations, he was a willing worker, for a good wage, save when the craving for liquor overtook him.

Keogh made another circle of the house. There were no sounds, which was as much a warning as reassurance. The hunt for him had drifted away, but it was not so distant but that night prowlers sensed peril and kept to cover.

There was no other door, no other way in or out. Keogh reached the sleeping guard, lifted an arm and struck him with a clubbed gun. The snore ended in mid-rasp, and the little man sighed, slumping more heavily in his chair, his head sagging. He did not move as Keogh dragged the chair to one side.

He'd be out for a while, but beyond a swollen cranium and a headache when he awoke, should suffer no ill effects.

The door was locked, but Keogh found a key ring in the guard's pocket. One key let him in.

Inside, the laboratory smell was much stronger. Not risking a light, Keogh prowled stealthily. One room was unquestionably a workshop.

He was looking in when he heard a door open behind him. He swung about, to see the Professor standing in bare feet and a long nightgown. In one hand he held a leveled revolver.

15.

The silence was like that of a clock, giving a preliminary whir, seemingly about to strike, then perversely dragging out the seconds. Though poor, the light was sufficient for eyes accustomed to the gloom. Keogh did not make the mistake of moving suddenly.

The Professor did not appear to be surprised.

"So!" he said. "It is you, the one they call Keogh, who has made fools of many, upsetting plans. You are here at the center of things. These fools do not the obvious see."

The gun was held steady in his hand. He waited as if expecting a reaction, then nodded thoughtfully.

"You are an intruder, a housebreaker. So I would justified be in shooting you. Is there any reason why I should not?"

"Several," Keogh returned. "I could let you out of here, for one thing."

"Out of here, maybe, but out of the valley—no. That much I could do, if I liked." He glanced meaningfully at the gun in hand. "In any case, why should

I wish to go? My great experiment approaches its climax. Do you take me for a fool?"

The question was more a statement and held a note of finality. As Keogh had guessed, this man was watched, guarded against his appetite for whiskey, but he was not really held against his will. Keogh had no doubt but that he knew how to use the gun, and would. He'd watch a man die with clinical detachment.

"You'll like the other reasons," Keogh assured him. "I've brought you several of them."

He held out a hand which clutched a bottle of whiskey. A sudden, avid light came into the Professor's eyes, increasing almost to a glare as a second bottle appeared in Keogh's other hand with a suggestion of a conjuring trick.

"I have four more to go with these," Keogh added. "It's the sort of stuff that your bosses drink—whenever they feel like it."

The Professor's breath was fast and uneven. He took a step forward, then paused warily.

"Give it to me."

Keogh shook his head. "Put up your gun first."

"You are a fool. I can kill you—just by a squeeze, a little pressure on the trigger."

"Nothing to stop you," Keogh conceded. "But I'll make sure that both these bottles smash as I go down." He waited a moment, then added softly. "And you wouldn't find the others."

The Professor considered that, striving to weigh the consequences against his desire, but the latter was too strong. Having had a taste that merely whetted his craving, he was desperate for the liquor.

"You are not so big a fool as the others," he granted, and shoved the revolver toward a pocket which was not there. Recollecting his attire, he turned back, tossing the gun onto a bed in the room behind.

"Now give me the bottles," he said, and clutched them as Keogh held them out. His eyes glittered with excitement.

"Now the others—you said there were six."

"There are. You get the others—if you're willing to tell me what you're doing back in here."

Keogh could see the struggle in the man's face as he considered the liquor already in hand. He shook his head.

"This will do. I am not a fool."

"Then why work for fools?" Keogh challenged. "I heard you say that was what they are."

"I do not talk, no. You have your freedom to go, I have these in exchange, so it is better that you go. One shout—and who would be then the fool?"

The logic was undeniable. And it was as much as Keogh had hoped for. The Professor, with some special particular skill, played an important part in what was going on. He might be needed again, very likely would be. But with plenty of whiskey in his possession—

"You win," Keogh agreed. "I'll get the other bottles."

By the time he returned with them, the Professor had one bottle opened and was drinking deeply, as though it were water. Keogh let himself out again, locked the door, and returned the key to the pocket where he had found it. He had a hunch that the guard, on awakening, might be a sadly puzzled man.

Uncertainly Keogh pondered his next move. Several hours of darkness remained, and it was vital to make good use of them. The problem of how that might be done bothered him. He had to think about Curt and Betty. Clearly she had been badly frightened of something which she probably was far from understanding, but she had followed them despite her fears, trying to warn them of the peril into which they were venturing. Apparently she had seen the course they followed and, knowing something of the secret of this valley, had guessed at the rest.

Her good intentions had made matters worse, but she deserved a lot of credit for trying to help.

If he could get out of the valley, he might enlist the help of his old friends, Whipple, Tone and O'Malley. They had formerly worked there, and their knowledge of the country would be valuable. But it was apparent that they knew that something was going on and were not anxious to be involved. In any case, getting out of the well-guarded valley would take a lot of doing.

The restlessness of the cattle in the corrals had not entirely subsided. Some had bedded down for the night, but many refused to accept captivity as right or proper. It would take some unusual circumstance to keep them awake and uneasy.

Weaning time, when calves were separated from their mothers, and branding time brought comparable distress to a herd. Neither situation would explain this disturbance.

These cattle, held in the several corrals, must have been rounded up and were presumably being held for shipment. But was their uneasiness caused by some experiment being conducted by the Professor? Keogh reached one corral and peered through the bars.

There was not much to see. A few of the herd were lying down, but most of them remained on their feet, restless and lowing.

Something caught Keogh's attention, a reflected gleam of moonlight. An object was inside the corral, close to the bars. He reached for it; it was half buried in dirt.

It was a sort of hypodermic needle, similar to ones he had seen before. Ranchers sometimes used such needles to insert a pill under the skin, inoculating their stock against the threat of blackleg. The disease, if it broke out in a herd, could kill dozens or scores, even hundreds, almost overnight.

Perhaps these cattle had been treated before being

shipped out. It was a possibility, but somehow the answer did not quite add up. If they were to be immunized, as would be reasonable in the case of such a valuable herd, it should have been done long before. Besides, except for a painful twinge when the needle was thrust under the skin and the pill driven in, they would suffer no discomfort.

Apparently this needle had been dropped, then lost in the dirt. There might be an answer here, but he had no way of knowing what it was.

This was another night in which he'd get no sleep, but Pratt was not concerned by the lack of slumber. There would be plenty of chance for that a little later. Events were moving, almost as if of their own accord, to the climax he had worked toward, and that was fine. Word had just come that the cattle cars, promised for several days but delayed in arrival, were finally on hand.

Pratt, already on his way to the valley, increased his pace. There was much to be done.

"Get the Professor," he instructed, and listened with only half his attention to the latest reports of what had happened in the valley during the evening. "We'll tend to Keogh in due time. Right now, the Professor has a job to do, 'fore these cattle can be shipped."

The report which came back, that the Professor had a stock of liquor and was in an ugly, uncooperative mood, threw him into a rage.

"Drunk, is he?" Pratt raged. "Well, this is one time he'll work, whiskey or no whiskey." He confronted the Professor, striding forward to jerk a bottle away from him.

"The herd's got to be doped tonight," he said harshly. "Do you hear—*tonight!* After it's done, you can make as big a hog of yourself as you like. But do your work first."

The Professor confronted him, bleary-eyed. "Give me that bottle!"

Pratt's answer was to smash it against the far wall.

"It'll be your thick head next," he warned, "unless you do as I tell you. Do you think I've come this far —to this point—to allow anything or anybody to spoil my plan? I'll use a hot iron on you if necessary, a branding iron, anything!"

The Professor sobered somewhat. His eyes were dark with hate.

"I need the whiskey if I'm to work," he pleaded.

"Not a drop till you finish," Pratt said flatly. "After that, all you want."

Helpless, the Professor gathered up his equipment and followed the others out into the night.

16.

The night was busier than most days; a good-sized crew was at work in and about the corrals. Keogh watched, aware that something portentous was taking place but unable to do anything about it. The cattle cars had arrived, and the herd were to be moved to the railroad and loaded on the train, starting at sunup. Apparently the cars had come unexpectedly, speeding up preparations by at least a day or so.

There was no longer any room for doubt as to who the boss was, the man who planned and was a driving force in executing the plans. Pratt was everywhere, supervising, encouraging, overseeing. Lanterns swung from the branches of trees or the topmost poles of corrals. Big bonfires added their light. The cattle were in an uneasy mood, but helpless to prevent what was happening to them.

Several groups were at work, shuttling them from one corral to another through narrow chutes where they could be handled with a minimum of trouble. The Professor, his face haggard, was kept busy filling an array of hypodermic needles, watching as others administered a dose to each animal, according to direction. The entire herd was being inoculated, preparatory to being shipped out.

But why, and for what, Keogh could not discover. If anyone save Pratt and the Professor knew, they were not talking or asking questions. It was as though they preferred not to know the answer.

Almost certainly this was not a dosage for black-leg. That could have been given long since. The timing, just before shipment, was ominous. There was something here as spooky and chilling as the ghost of the Folly.

Keogh was suddenly appalled, uncertain how to proceed. Despite the size of the crew at work, the gates and the creek were still watched. Pratt was taking no chances of any last-minute failure. He had planned long and carefully for something, and he was demonstrating cleverness as well as ruthlessness.

Looks as though this time you've bitten off more than you can chew, Keogh told himself grimly. Choke on it, and you die—and so do a lot of others!

He had seen enough here, and he moved away from the corrals, for once unable to come up with a promising idea. The night would soon be gone. He might hole up somewhere and hide out the day, but that would allow Pratt to put his plan into final operation.

Action was called for, and he was one man, and

only one, caught in a trap. What had seemed during the afternoon like a fairly simple and safe bit of exploration had boomeranged.

Something loomed blacker than its surroundings, and he made out the outlines of another cabin. It was nearly a mile from either of the others, and there was a difference. It was set against the side of a steep hill, and sheer chance or luck had directed his steps to where it might be seen. Normally, the trees and brush which grew close, as well as the contour of the surrounding hills, would hide it.

Such concealment had clearly been planned, rather than being a matter of chance. This place was patterned after a farmer's root cellar, dug back into the side of the hill. Only the front, of heavy logs, was visible, catching the moonlight for a brief period. Examination showed a stout door, but no windows.

Curt and Betty might have been brought there. Whether they had or not was worth finding out.

A well-trodden path indicated that the place received a lot of useage.

A padlock was slipped into a heavy hasp on the door, but it had not been shut, attesting to the confidence that no one would bother to enter. Or it might be that the room held nothing of value.

Keogh swung the door open. It rasped on unoiled hinges, and heavy air hit him like a blow. Beyond was a solid pit of blackness.

Somewhere, something stirred uncertainly in the

gloom. Keogh took a chance.

"Who's in there?"

There was a silence, as though the question were being thought over, evaluated. Then a counter question came, in a voice hoarse with doubt and dawning hope.

"Who are *you?*"

"A friend," Keogh returned. "If you're a prisoner, come on out. I can't take time now to explain, but there's a lot going on."

Again there was a moment of hesitation; then someone groped toward him and through the door into the dimness of the night. Even that, Keogh realized, might still seem bright to one who had been confined in such a black pit.

"Anyone else in there?" Keogh asked. "Or anything you want?"

The other man was taking hope and regaining confidence at the prospect of freedom. This time he answered more readily.

"Nobody else. And there's nothing I want from that hole. Who are you? What's going on?"

Keogh closed the door and snapped the lock in place, then led the way back from the cellar.

"Speak soft," he warned. "The place is swarming with an obnoxious crew. I'd be pleased to know your name."

"I'm Curt Jackson, owner of this ranch. Or I'm supposed to be," he added bitterly.

Keogh observed that his face was covered by whiskers or several weeks' growth. The cloth he wore appeared to have gone long unchanged.

"How long have you been shut up in there?"

"How long? Forever, it seems like. I've lost count of time. In such a hole, there's no difference between day or night. It must have been months, I guess." He was about to say more, but Keogh cut in with another question:

"Who put you there?"

A touch of pride still remained in the man. Even such treatment as he had endured had not broken his spirit.

"It took half a dozen men to do it. Pratt was the one who gave the orders, if that's what you mean."

That fitted in with other developments. Keogh nodded.

"I'm known as Keogh," he explained. "I'm in this section to investigate what's going on. I'm beginning to get a pretty good idea, though there's still a lot that I don't savvy. I suppose Pratt made you some sort of a proposition?"

"Yeah, he came to me a year or more ago and wanted to buy my place, my herd of pure-bred Herefords along with the land. He offered me a good price, but it was to be paid sometime in the future. Knowing him, I figured it was crooked, and I'd be left holding the sack. Not that I wanted to sell, anyhow. He kept pestering me, and finally I told him to go to the devil. Then the next thing I knew, I was shut up in there."

"From what I know of him, you're lucky to be alive," Keogh observed. "Perhaps he's kept you with the notion of having you sign some legal papers, or something."

"I expect that's the reason I was kept alive," Jackson conceded. "He called on me a couple of times, and asked if I was willing to show some sense and sign everything over to him—supposedly as a pardner. I wasn't willing, and he said I could stay in there till I got some sense. The second time he warned me that if I kept on being stubborn, I might be left to rot. By then, though, I'd remembered where I'd seen him before. He'd been a convict, a lifer, and I knew I couldn't trust him. If I'd signed, it'd have been my death warrant."

A keeper had brought him food once a day. With the meal would come a match and a small length of candle. The light would last long enough for him to eat, but not much more. The rest of the time he had been alone with darkness and loneliness, treatment calculated to break his will to resist.

Since he was supposed to be somewhere in the East, and Pratt was now accepted as a partner, in charge of the operation, there had been no pressing need for haste. He had been held a prisoner, while Pratt made use of the valley for the furtherance of his own plans. Keogh suspected that it was a part of the saloon-keeper's scheme to fasten the guilt on Jackson, as the real owner.

Insofar as he understood it, Keogh gave a brief résumé of the situation. He explained how they had found the old road, the underwater bridge which led up from the wild fastnesses of the Folly. Jackson listened in astonishment.

"I never knew anything about that," he protested. "From what you say, it sounds as though that road and bridge must have been there for a year or more. But I sure didn't suspect any such thing."

"It adds up," Keogh agreed, "including those rustled herds, which must have been held back in the valley."

"I didn't know about those, either," Jackson insisted. "But I can see how it might have happened. My wife got mighty sick, maybe a year before Pratt really started pestering me, though he had tried to buy. She was so bad off, I took her East, to the best doctors I could find." His voice grew tight.

"I stayed right there with her as long as she lived. I can see now that my being gone gave Pratt plenty of chance to do about as he pleased around here. I know that there were traitors among my crew, who sold out to him. I was beginning to realize that something was stinkin' when I got back the second time, and Pratt made what he called his final offer, then jumped me as I've told you."

Keogh had no doubt that Jackson was telling the

truth. That explained much which until then had been obscure. Pratt had seen the opportunity, had made his plans, and had taken over. Circumstances, particularly the fact Jackson had been away so much, had played into his hands, been a break in his favor. But Pratt would probably have managed in any case.

The saloon with the adjoining hotel in town, even the robbery of unsuspecting guests at the hotel, was in itself a carefully planned part of the operation, an elaborate cover for a larger scheme. Pratt knew that people suspected him of petty crimes and worked to spread that reputation. It would not occur to them that a man who indulged in such penny-ante pursuits could be the brains back of the rustling and larger crimes which had plagued the country.

Even the rustling was only a smoke screen to hide something bigger and more sinister. Yet what Pratt really aimed at he still could not be sure.

Questioned on that point, Jackson could offer no help. He had wondered if the valley was used to hide the stolen herds, though moving them in and out along the one road and main gate had appeared to him to be an almost insuperable obstacle.

He had supposed that Pratt intended to steal both his land and his valuable herd of blooded stock, and sooner or later, he would try to force Jackson to sign everything over to him. He had counted on time and the black loneliness of the prison to produce this result.

"One sure thing: he's in full control here now, with a crew that he can depend on," Keogh said grimly. "Any who were loyal to you have been weeded out." He outlined the operation which was even then taking place, the apparent inoculation of the herd which were to be shipped out that day.

"Counting all the hands he has on Hendricks' ranch, as well as here, including extra men from town, he has what amount to an army," Keogh admitted. "We've got to stop him—but right now, I'm fresh out of any ideas that hold any prospect of working."

Jackson was equally at a loss as to how to proceed.

"Sounds like we need an army of our own," he said wryly. "If we could get word to the major at the post and have him come with his men, that might do it. But the chance of either of us getting out of here to carry word is almost as poor as it was for me when I was shut up in there. I made a few tries when they brought my dinner, but it never worked. With as big a crew as you say he has, there'll be men on watch, the gate locked, and the creek off south guarded, too. A man *might* swim it, with luck, but if you got across, you'd be afoot. And Pratt will probably have other guards on watch down there."

Pratt had dourly complained that the Folly was worthless, but he had refused to risk it on a throw of the dice. His reasons were understandable, and the picture which Jackson painted was gloomy. Still, going by that route was a possibility. The difficulty was that traveling on foot would require a lot more time than was likely to be at their disposal.

Daylight was on the way, a splash of crimson across the east heralding the sun, and all at once the valley was openly astir. Apparently the work of inoculating the cattle had been completed. Now the herd was being spilled out from the corrals, lined into one bunch and started toward the main gate and the road beyond. By sunset, the herd should be on the cattle cars, ready for shipment and transshipment to most parts of the country. Having made his plans well in advance of this key date, Pratt was not allowing anything to disrupt his timetable.

Every crew member would be on the watch for any sign of Jackson or himself, but Pratt was confident that they could do nothing which might interfere. To show themselves would mean being captured or shot.

It was sunup now, and the herd was on the move. At least a score of cowboys made sure that they headed straight, with no straying. As many more riders were visible at strategic points, every man heavily armed.

"What we need—" Jackson sighed gloomily—"is a miracle. And I can't figure out no way of conjurin' one up."

17.

Fear is a common affliction, a heritage from ancient times, when men crouched at the mouth of a cave, striving with a flimsy spear of wood, tipped by flint, to hold off a ravening beast.

Hendricks had stumbled in its shadow too long a time, until he came to start at shadows. The way had scarcely been made more palatable by the countering force of greed. Now the shadows had grown long?

.It was not that he'd chosen such a course from choice or of his own free will. He'd been working as an honest man, though fighting a losing battle to build up a small outfit, to make a living for his family. Pratt had appeared at a critical juncture, appearing somewhat like a cross between angel and devil. In his hands, as in those of justice, Pratt had balanced a scale and exhibited it to Hendricks, with greed on the one side and fear on the other.

"You can be rich almost without turnin' a hand," he'd suggested. "Or you can lose what little you've got—and you know what you have that counts big for you." Though subtle, the threat had carried the prickle of fear. "We're old friends," Pratt had added, a term with such doubtful connotations that Hendricks had shivered.

A man should be allowed one mistake, especially if he heartily repented of it; Hendricks had assured himself of that many times over the years. The trouble was that the mistake had not been paid for, in the eyes of the law. Also, it was known to Pratt—the only man Hendricks had encountered in nearly a score of years who remembered.

Actually it had seemed merely a slight mistake, an error in judgment. He had allowed himself to be persuaded to hold a few saddled horses for friends, while they settled a quarrel with a rival crew in a saloon. That was what they'd told him, and he, being a tenderfoot in more ways than one, had swallowed the story. They had explained that they might be out-numbered and forced to run for it, so they wanted to have the horses ready for a quick getaway.

The quarrel had turned out to be the robbery of a bank. A couple of men had been killed, and by the time Hendricks understood what was going on, he had found himself a captive, one of the gang. Shortly thereafter he'd been behind penitentiary walls.

Half a year later, with a score of years of his sentence still to be served, he'd virtually been dragged to freedom in a jail-break, of which he'd had no knowledge until it happened. After that he'd been a fugitive, a man with a price on his head.

Traveling to a new range, he'd built a new life on the ruins of the old, finally risking marriage, working hard but without much success. He had come to regard the past as no more than a bad dream when Pratt had turned up, offering him a far better ranch than the one he possessed, of which he would appear to be the owner, and a prosperous life. There had been temptation on the one side and a threat on the other, and he had not dared to refuse.

It hadn't been too bad at first, even the selling of a herd to the Army, a herd promptly stolen from the post by Indians, and later returned to him almost intact. The new brand which the cattle wore assured his safety, or so Pratt had pointed out. To Hendricks, its similarity with the old one was like a pointing finger. But by then the jaws of the trap had closed.

He'd realized, as in the bank robbery, that Pratt was up to something a lot bigger than the stealing of one bunch of cattle; he was being used to distract attention from Pratt, to focus suspicion upon himself.

Hendricks stood barefooted in the middle of the floor, shaking with anger and apprehension. The former became predominant as he understood what he was being told and grasped the implications. Betty had gone north and vanished.

She was his daughter, and he knew that she had sensed the fear, the suspicion and its implications, and perhaps had come to understand too much. Also, she had given her love to a man, perhaps too fast and unreasonably, but surely. Hendricks couldn't blame her too much for that. Curt was a personable fellow, and Betty had had few opportunities to know such men. Also, love was not a matter of reason, but of the heart. It had been that way with him and Betty's mother.

Now, because she had tried to help Curt, fearful that he was venturing into forbidden territory, she was herself a prisoner in that unchancy valley to the north. Probably by now she was a captive of the man who also held him in bond.

Hendricks was trembling as he tugged on his boots. Fear had given way to fury. If he took a hand it might spell ruin, but for once, he was beyond caring for himself.

He hesitated as he let himself out into the night, given pause by a grim reflection. As far as the public knew, he was the owner there, boss of the crew asleep in the adjoining bunk house. But the unsettling fact was that those men were employed by Pratt and paid by him, and they knew that as well as he did. They liked Betty and they might feel sorry for her, but they wouldn't follow him in a rescue attempt—not against the boss.

Keogh—but Keogh and Curt were up there also, and by now they were prisoners as well. If they were not in actual captivity, it amounted to the same thing. Hendricks knew the valley, which was literally a prison, and the numbers on the other side were overwhelming.

There might be one chance, albeit a slender one.

Hendricks rode hard toward town. It did not occur to him that an army might not only be required, but might perhaps be recruited. Hendricks was pretty well convinced in his own mind that the headstrong commandant at the post would clap him in the guardhouse, should he have the temerity to show his face there.

The three listened incredulously to Hendricks, then agreed to ride with him. It was Fred Whipple who came up with a plan. Keogh was their friend; also, they were tired of doing nothing, were eager for a bit of excitement. But they had ridden only a short distance before they slowed down, realizing that riding headlong against a stone wall, or into a trap, would do no one any good. They needed something more if they were to circumvent the odds against them.

Daylight had come by then. Whipple pointed.

"Look yonder. They're starting to bring the herd out through the gate and head for the stockyards. I understand the cattle cars are there, ready for loading."

The others viewed the activity hopefully. "Maybe we could sneak in among the herd and through the gate without them noticin'," Zeke Tone suggested, but his voice was doubtful rather than hopeful.

Whipple shook his head. "Not a chance. There'd be

riflemen guardin' that gate every second—and they'd
stop us sure. We ain't too popular around here any
more. But I know a path back in the hills. Call it a
trail. I climbed part of it one day, followin' a puma
I'd shot. I never did tell anybody about that route,
but I got pretty well up it from the inside, and maybe
—just maybe—we can go down it. It's a chance, if
you ain't too worried about a broken neck."

The others were in a mood to take a chance, though
his designation of the route as a trail caused head-
shaking as they followed his lead. It required circling and climbing among the mountains, then, when
finally the crest was attained, a winding, treacherous
descent which left the horses snorting and uneasy. By
then there was another impelling motive for keeping
on. Once started down that path, there was no turning
back. It was too narrow, too steep. A horse simply
could not turn around.

Sweating and hard-breathing, they found themselves in the valley. With so many of the crew occupied with the cattle, no one had discovered their
unorthodox entrance.

"All we've got to do now is find Curt and Keogh
and your daughter—then set them loose, if they're
prisoners, and get out." O'Malley grinned, and swiped
a shirt-sleeve across his sweat-beaded face. "If they
are prisoners, they'll likely be held at one of the
cabins back in mid-valley, or maybe in that old root
cellar that's stood empty for years."

They rode openly now, figuring they would be less likely to attract attention than by furtive movements; also, time was at a premium.

Hearing the sound of hoofs, Keogh looked, stared an instant in surprise, then stepped into view. For the first time in hours, he was able to grin.

"You're about the last fellows I hoped to set eyes on, but I won't say it's not a pleasure," he greeted them.

To Hendricks' urgent question, he had no positive answer.

"They grabbed Betty last night, and Curt rushed to her rescue—and got caught, too," he admitted. "I don't have any idea where they're being held. I've been hunting more or less ever since, but Jackson is the only prisoner I've come up with."

"They've got to be found," Hendricks insisted. "That comes ahead of everything else."

Keogh was in agreement, though the miracle for which Jackson had wished seemed unlikely. True, there were six of them now, and if they could find and free Betty and Curt, they would number eight. But to force an escape from the valley, against odds of six or eight to one, with a barred gate and other obstacles in the way, would still be almost out of the question.

If they succeeded in finding and rescuing the captives, an alarm would be sounded, and immediate pursuit would follow. By day, the odds would lie with their pursuers. To escape by the precarious path the four had taken in entering would be out of the question. Riflemen below could pick them off at leisure.

"Too bad you didn't think to get word to Major Tombright," Keogh observed. "He'd have come with the Army—and the Army's what we need right now."

Hendricks was as surprised as he was shocked at the notion.

"Gosh," he confessed, "I didn't think of that. The major has a theory that I'm some shades darker than a horse thief, and if I was to show up at the post, I expect that he'd be in a mood to do something unpleasant."

Knowing the impetuous nature of Tombright, as well as his rancor, Keogh was forced to agree that Hendricks' apprehensions might be justified. In any case, the opportunity had been missed.

They discussed the situation, Keogh filling the newcomers in on the Professor and other details. He told how Curt and himself had first found the body of Runs Like a Wolf, which drew a surprised rejoinder from Hendricks.

"So that's what happened to the Indian, eh?" he asked. "I counted him as sort of a friend, and I've wondered about him. He just disappeared, and nobody ever did figure out why." He colored uncomfortably.

"I might as well admit what I guess you know by now anyhow, Keogh. Pratt owns my spread and everything on it. I'm just a hired hand, servin' as a front for him—and so suspicion is fixed on me instead of him, as I've come to see. When that herd was stolen, Pratt hired some of the Indians to do the job. It was an exciting chance for wild young bucks who weren't allowed to take the war trail any more, and he paid them with whiskey.

"And of course, if they'd been caught, they'd have been the ones to suffer, not him. Pratt didn't expose himself, but worked through an agent, same as he usually does. Runs Like a Wolf suspected what was up, and he didn't like it. I'm sure of that much. He must have set out to discover just what was going on— and from the looks of things, he learned more than it was healthy to know."

That was much as Keogh had suspected. For his pains, Runs Like a Wolf had received a bullet in the back. Badly hurt, he'd gotten as far as the old packing plant and crawled inside to die. And like a number of others, he was still unavenged.

The bad part was that, despite this addition to their forces, the basic situation was unchanged. The herd was outside the gate now, on the way to the railroad, but they were still inside, their situation little different from the one in which the Pawnee had found himself.

This was a breathing spell. And if a sudden shout of alarm was any indication, their period of grace was swiftly drawing to a close.

18.

Pratt was in an expansive mood. There had been
setbacks and risks, but his meticulous planning had
paid off, and would continue to do so in the days and
weeks to come. He was well on the way to realizing
the vengeance to which he had dedicated his life; a
revenge so sweeping, so devastating, that it would
virtually encompass the entire country, not just a few
foes. Nothing could stop him now.

He'd driven the Professor to complete his task,
standing over him with a drawn gun as the Professor
grew more and more sullen or tried to loiter, clipping
him alongside the head with the barrel of his revolver
when additional persuasion was needed. He'd empha-
sized who was boss, and now that job was done. The
drunken hog could swill his whiskey as much as he
liked. What he did or did not do no longer mattered.

If he stayed drunk long enough and hung around
the country, he'd be caught and hanged. Probably he
was too dumb to understand or realize. That would be

a fitting reward for what he'd done.

As soon as the cattle were loaded on the train, Pratt would pull out, too, riding off into the night and vanishing. When his vengeance struck, he would be far from the valley, where no one would think of looking.

Hearing a shout, Pratt swung to join a suddenly gathering bunch of his crew, and this time he actually smiled. Keogh and Jackson were surrounded, cut off, along with Hendricks and three of his former crew. Hendricks had chosen to play a fool's part, so he would deserve what he got. The others, who had worked for Jackson, had refused his offer when he had taken over. Their capture was a final fillip.

He hoped the six might be foolish enough to go for their guns, to attempt a desperate, last-ditch resistance. But with the odds as long as they were, and nowhere to run even if they should temporarily break loose, the others followed Keogh's example and surrendered meekly. Pratt ran his tongue across his lips.

"You showed good sense, not fighting back," he admitted grudgingly. "I can think of a better way for men to die than by bullets."

His words could have been a comment on the situation, but they had more the sound of a threat.

The decision to submit, rather than make a fight of it, was one of the hardest Keogh had ever been called upon to make. The realization that it might lead to disaster plagued him, but the certainty that all of them would die if they resisted stayed his hand. As long as a man lived he could hope, but only while he lived.

They were quickly disarmed, then herded off to another house which Keogh had not seen before. Built of heavy logs, it was a substantial prison, and the cellar underneath looked as escape-proof as the one in which Curt Jackson had been confined. In it, they found Curt and Betty, who greeted them unhappily.

"You, too, Keogh?" Curt asked. "Somehow I got the idea that you always had an ace in the hole when it was really needed; that you could out-think even Pratt."

"I'm sorry to disappoint you," Keogh replied. "I'm disappointed in myself."

Perhaps because Betty was a woman, their captors had made one concession to their comfort. That was a lantern which gave enough light to temper the darkness if not completely to dissipate the gloom. It showed their prison to be windowless, with only one heavy door, barred on the outside.

Presently the dor was opened and a substantial breakfast brought in by well-armed guards.

"The boss said to give you a good feed," one of the messengers explained jovially. "You know how it is: a condemned man always gets a last meal. The Chink sort of outdid himself on this."

"You don't mean that," Betty protested. "You're just trying to frighten us."

"Not you, ma'am," the guard protested. "I don't reckon you've anything to be apprehensive about. Anyhow, you might as well enjoy your food."

A second meal was brought them later in the day. Nothing else broke the monotony. Then the thing they had both feared and hoped for happened, as the door was thrown open, letting in a last glimpse of sunlight. It revealed at least half a dozen guards, watchful against any rash attempt to escape. One shouted an order!

"Keogh! You and your pardner—come on out!"

Suddenly terrified, Betty clung to Curt.

"Don't go! They'll kill you! I know that he's planned something dreadful for you and Mr. Keogh! Don't go!"

In confirmation, the foreman answered sardonically:

"Would you rather have him shot in your arms, lady? Better take them from around his neck and let him come."

As she did not obey, he eared back the hammer on his rifle and sighted along the barrel. Despairingly, Betty released Curt, then strove to follow as the two were taken out. The guards posted at the door barred her way.

"The boss sent word that you was to be let out in about another hour, girl," he said. "Then you can go home if you want to. And the rest of you can spend the night here. Tomorrow you can go outside, though you'll have to stay in the valley a few days longer."

Such reassurance as might lie in his words was offset by the implied threat. At the door, Keogh's hands were jerked in back of him; Curt received the same treatment. Then they were helped onto horses and taken away, still under heavy escort.

For once, neither could find anything to say. It was only too apparent that this was slated to be their last ride.

"You fellows made two mistakes," one of the guards informed them. "The first was to come snooping—and the second was to do too good a job."

Not much to Keogh's surprise, they went out through the big gate on the main road, then on toward the railroad. It was evening again, and the shadows were beginning to merge, flowing together into pools of blackness.

Keogh had napped during the day, but he was still tired. The distant bawling of the cattle reached their ears, growing louder as they neared the still raw grade of the railroad, the freshly peeled logs of the stockyards. The sound was troubled and disconsolate, as though the cattle too sensed that their destination would be marked with a large D for disaster.

The cattle train stretched away in the dusk, more than half a hundred cars on a side-track, already loaded, each car filled to capacity. A few stragglers were being shoved along a chute and into the last car as they approached. Besides the cowboys, sweating at their task, other men sat on horses and watched from the shadows. This was a well-disciplined crew. The gun-hawks who headed it obeyed orders, asking no questions.

Aside from these grim watchers, no others were around. Townspeople and ranchers had come out during the day to watch the loading, an event which marked a milestone in the community's history. Even a week before, the stockyards had not been erected; the first scheduled train was yet to essay the new twin lines of steel. Never before had anything of the sort happened in that land. All at once, vast distances were being bridged, distant markets brought within reach.

The operation had the outward appearance of progress. Thoroughbred cattle were being sold and shipped in businesslike fashion. None of the onlookers had been disturbed or harassed or given any reason to suppose that a more sinister operation was taking place before their eyes.

Finally, tiring at day's end and with their curiosity satisfied, the onlookers had drifted away. Only then had Keogh and Curt been brought there.

At the far end of the line, a locomotive puffed and wheezed, smoke belching from the broad stack, moving the train ahead a car length at a time, on signal, to allow the loading of each. When that was completed, and the caboose hooked onto the rear, all that remained was to close the door on the last car. Such

men as were going along to look after the cattle would
enter the caboose, and the train would roll eastward.

The last reluctant cow was hazed and prodded up
the chute and on board. Only then did Pratt emerge
from the gloom, mounted on a horse as dark as its
surroundings. It was not too dark to see the sardonic
smile of satisfaction on his face.

"Tie them to that post temporarily," he instructed.
"Run a rope around the post and the two of them.
Then the rest of you get back out of the way. I've a
few partin' remarks for the ears of these two, to sort
of sweeten their last moments, you might say."

A stout snubbing post was conveniently at hand. A
couple of turns of a lariat, around the post and themselves, held them securely as the others drew back as
ordered. Pratt chuckled dryly.

"You've worked hard to find out what was going
on, so I reckon you might as well know, now that it's
too late to make any difference anyhow," he explained. "You made a fool of me a couple of times,
so I'm returnin' the compliment.

"I've worked a long while for a fitting vengeance—
and I've got it. You noticed how the cattle were being
given shots last night—like we were inoculating them
against blackleg. Only this time we weren't inoculating them against anything, but for something."

The saddle leather creaked as he shifted position.

"I guess it's never been done before, but I got the
notion, and I didn't see why it couldn't be worked

out. The Professor is a trained vet, but he's a lot more than that—and a mighty smart man when he's sober. And like me, he holds a grudge against the world, so he was plenty willing to do what I wanted—special in exchange for a good round sum, and a safe place away from the law while he worked.

"It took quite a while and a lot of experimentin', but he worked it out, down to the right dosage to give and the time it takes the stuff to act."

At the far end of the train, the locomotive whistled, a questioning blast. Pratt refused to be hurried.

"The Jackson Ranch, with its pedigreed Herefords, was just what the doctor ordered—meaning me. There's close to two thousand head here, to be sent out and transshipped to every part of the country. After they're all delivered, they'll sicken and die— and spread a trail of plague and disaster to sweep the nation!"

"This ain't blackleg—though that's bad enough. But this is worse. You'll have heard about it, Keogh; maybe you've even seen it. Hoof and mouth."

He raised his voice, swinging his horse.

"All right, boys. Load them in with the rest of the cattle."

Promptly the guards appeared, loosening the rope which held them to the snubbing post and shoving them up the chute. At the door, open just wide enough for a man to crowd through, their bonds were slashed; then they were shoved inside and the door slammed shut.

Again the locomotive whistled, a long, mournful wail. Car by car, the train jerked into motion. The heavy breathing of the frightened, close-packed cattle came from all around, and a horn prodded Curt's shoulder as the car began to lurch.

19.

Keogh listened, appalled, though not particularly surprised. He had guessed part of what was going on, though the real answer, the revelation of the magnitude of the plot, was shocking. He and Curt had been almost in time, had come close to discovering the secret and putting a stop to the plot.

Almost. But Pratt had made his plans over a long span of years, revising and altering them, striving to foresee and guard against all contingencies. And now the herd was loaded, the train rolling—a herd doomed to death, carrying plague and destruction with it.

Blackleg was bad enough, a killer which, once started, could devastate whole herds, even ranges. Yet by comparison it was mild alongside hoof and mouth disease. Once these animals were introduced into other prize herds across the country, they would sicken. By the time their illness was diagnosed, others would be infected,

The scourge of so widespread a disease might virtually wipe out the cattle industry across the country. There was no known remedy, short of killing and burying or burning whole herds, every infected animal and those suspected of infection. Even after the plague had run its course, the virus would linger for years in the ground, rendering vast areas unsafe for further use.

Pratt was by way of wreaking vengeance on a staggering scale.

The train was picking up speed, wheels clicking, the cars beginning to sway with the motion. It had been too dark to see, but Keogh suspected that a couple of locomotives were pulling the train. Normally, they'd run through the night and until some time the next day before making a halt. Cattle trains were usually given the right of way above all others, including passenger runs.

Once each day they would stop some place where ample facilities were available for caring for the cattle. All the animals would be unloaded, given time to move about, to eat and drink, then herded back into the cars and the journey resumed.

At some stop, the train would be broken up, some cars shunted west, south or east and attached to other trains. The advertising campaign, the careful selection of orders, was insurance that the plague, when it developed, would not be localized.

At the moment, the cattle inside the car were as

tired and apprehensive, as a result of the unusual events of the last few days, as were the two-legged captives. They were packed in as tightly as possible, partly to make use of all available shipping space, and in part so that it was almost impossible for an animal to fall with the lurching of the train. Once down, an animal rarely managed to get back on its feet. It would be trampled and killed.

That, Curt and Keogh realized, was the fate Pratt planned for them. They had humiliated him in public, threatening the success of his cherished plan, so no ordinary death would do. Pratt lived for vengeance, and they were something very special in the way of potential victims.

Like the cattle, they were locked in, and even if their shouts could have been heard above the noise of the train and the bawling of the cattle, there would be no one to hear.

As soon as the strangeness began to wear off and the cattle grew accustomed to the motion, they would become restless and try to move about. Then, rendered more impatient when they found it impossible, they would feel a sullen resentment. Scenting man, whom they counted responsible for all their troubles, they would turn hostile. Men on horseback they understood and accepted, but men on foot they distrusted without fearing them.

Keogh had submitted to capture and manhandling without a struggle. Under a battery of watchful eyes and leveled guns, with hands tied behind his back, he had had scant choice. At least passive acceptance had kept them alive.

He understood Pratt's thinking. It wouldn't take long before the cattle, becoming more aware of the hated presence of men, savage from confinement and all the indignities of recent hours, would turn on them. Pratt had lived long enough in the country to know longhorn nature.

Apparently he'd classified all cattle in that category, and that might give the two men a chance. Longhorns were a half-wild breed, who as a strain had survived for generations by their ability to fight all enemies—packs of wolves, stalking grizzlies, blizzard and heat and drought. Their hatred for other creatures, including man, was instinctive.

Moreover, their horns were rapier-tipped and formidable. Herefords, particularly these pure-bred ones, were not so savage by training or instinct, and their horns were less than half the size of longhorns'.

Keogh tried to move along the side of the car. With the cattle packed as close as they were, that was not easy, but he managed a step or so without causing active resentment.

The open slats of the cattle car were not very wide, but he got an arm through. Straining, he managed to reach the latch of the door. Sensing what he was attempting, Curt was beside him, helping to keep stray horns from prodding or gouging. Keogh grunted.

"Locked," he observed without surprise. "Somebody snapped a padlock on this one—just in case. We have to give Pratt credit. He does a careful job of planning."

Curt had been afraid of that. In the last few hours he had come to entertain an unwilling respect for the man. He tried to keep despair from his voice.

"It was worth a try, anyhow."

"It still is," Keogh returned. A couple of times during the day he'd held his breath, first when they were disarmed, again when they were led out for this final journey. The first search had been reasonably thorough, but they had been satisfied on finding his holstered gun and a second one in a shoulder holster. They had not searched him again.

So he still had a hide-out weapon, carefully preserved against such an emergency. In that respect he was like Pratt, preferring to plan against all possible contingencies.

The gun was in a special holster down his back, suspended by a cord around his neck, under his clothes. It took some wriggling to get it out, but the short-barreled gun was fully loaded. Curt nodded as though not much surprised.

"You always manage to come up with an ace in the hole," he observed.

"Let's hope it will work," Keogh returned.

The difficulty in that cramped and crowded position, with his arm thrust through a slat and unable to see his target very well, was to make the shots count. He fired twice, and scored one hit against the padlock without weakening it. The second salvo of bullets both hit, but the lock remained stubborn. He was forced to empty the gun before the lock gave way.

The cattle were jumpy at the sound of the gun, but they tried to veer away instead of crowding. Keogh got his fingers on the broken lock and tossed it aside. To shove the door open even a little, in view of the cattle crowded against it, required his and Curt's combined strength. Finally he thrust his arms and shoulders through.

The train was really rolling, as though the engineer, impatient after the long day spent switching, moving cars only a few feet at a time, were anxious to make up for the delay. It rolled and swayed, and the new track, so very recently put in use over a new road bed, was rough and uneven. Keogh got a grip on the top slat, then dragged himself upward.

He stepped out, suspended in space, hanging for a moment, then pulled himself to the top of the car and sprawled flat. Reaching down, he lent a hand as Curt followed.

"Whoosh!" Curt expelled his breath, sinking down beside him. "I hardly expected to get out of there alive, Keogh."

"Loaded dice can work both ways," Keogh observed. "It's a lesson Pratt is slow to learn."

They got to their feet, balancing on the swaying car top, finding it little to their liking. It was one thing to ride a bucking horse, or even to climb or descend a dizzy trail along a mountainside, but trains were new in their experience. Never before had either been atop one as it surged through the night at what seemed not merely breath-taking but reckless speed.

"What next?" Curt asked.

"Guess we'd better pay a courtesy call on the engineer," Keogh decided; "sort of drop in on him, you might say." He reached for the brake wheel on top of the car, steadying himself. He added as an afterthought: "We'll set the brakes as we go along."

Curt was not adverse to anything which might slow the train. The plan seemed feasible until he realized that they were not to be allowed to put it into operation at their leisure. Something popped up at the rear of the car, peering like a coyote. A second head appeared beside it.

There was an exclamation, audible above the other noises, and Keogh, straightening after setting the brake, shouted for Curt to come on. He jumped the gap between cars, and in spite of the swaying and the uncertain footing, Curt was right at his heels.

Here was a development which neither had foreseen. Intent on getting out of the cattle car, they had forgotten that the caboose was right behind, with at least half a dozen men riding comfortably in it.

Some of them belonged to the train crew—at least the conductor and brakeman did. The others were from Pratt's crew, picked to make the trip, to help care for the cattle on the way. That was required by the railroad, though feeding and watering were less important than making sure that nothing should interfere with the train and the scheduled delivery of the cattle.

The shots had been heard. Since they had come in bursts of a couple of shots at a time, the suspicious crewmen had understood where they were from and what they meant. Keogh or Curt had a gun and was blasting the lock. Once out of the car, they'd get on top on the train.

The trainmen were ready to assist, even if they did not understand where the other men might have come from or what they were about. Men using guns must be up to mischief.

Now the crew were swarming from the caboose to the top of the cattle car. As Curt and Keogh fled, the others strung out in hot pursuit.

The trainmen were accustomed to such footing, but they were no more zealous than Pratt's gunmen. Understanding only too well the hazards involved, they were using their guns. In poor light and under such conditions, their targets were uncertain, but some bullets whistled uncomfortably close. It occurred to Curt that in a long chase the odds were all in favor of their pursuers, especially since the foremen and engineers at the front of the train would also be inclined to be hostile.

"How about slowing them a little by giving them a few shots in return?" he gasped.

Keogh's reply held no reassurance.

"Can't. My gun's empty—no more shells."

20.

For both Curt and Keogh it had been a day of extremes, alternating between depression and exultation. Until the night before, Curt had not dared give free scope even to dreams, for they had seemed hopelessly beyond reach. Whatever Hendricks might be, his daughter was wonderful, a quality which rendered her very desirable, but at the same time completely out of reach. Even apart from the fact that her father was a big cattleman, and that he was not a cattle buyer, the scope of his activities, if successful, could only serve to widen the already existing gulf between them.

Then all at once the object of his dreams had been at hand and in distress, and he had essayed, however ingloriously, the role of knight. Then they had been taken prisoner, and though both were captives, they were together. Under such circumstances, Curt had found the courage to admit what otherwise he would not have dared put into words—that she was his dream.

Impossibly, bewilderingly, she had confessed to loving him as well.

For a while, scarcely troubled by more mundane matters, he had walked on air. Now he was almost walking on air again, but with a difference. Plunging along in the darkness atop a narrow, swaying train, with bullets probing the air around him, was a fantastic climax to all that had gone before.

A slip or misstep could send him hurtling, with the probability he would break his neck when he hit the ground. That would almost certainly happen long before they could reach the front end of the train, barring a hit before then by a bullet.

Keogh bobbed like a shadow and was gone; then Curt followed, ducking down between two cars. He felt a rush of confidence, grasped for a ladder rung and rested one foot on the chattering coupling below. Trust Keogh to put on a good show! He'd fled just far enough to stir the excitement of the chase in their pursuers, who were coming hard at their heels.

Still clutching for support with one hand, Curt reached with the other, closing his fingers around an ankle as its owner started to jump the gap between cars. A wild yell, a banshee wail compounded of surprise, outrage and terror, was his response, one which could hardly inspire confidence among the rest of the group. Keogh was also busy, plucking like an otter among a flock of ducks.

Curt's captive, dragged into the recess, was struggling wildly. Curt twisted a gun away to use as a club, and was disappointed as his opponent jerked aside, then, yelling anew, spilled into the darkness at the side of the train.

What might have been a violent landing was tempered by the fact the train was coming to a jarring stop. Hearing the shooting and interpreting it as a sign of trouble, the engine men were halting the cars.

There was no time to give thought to this, for the sudden jerk dislodged Curt. He hit the ground, rolled, and came dizzily to his feet.

The shaken occupants of the cars were lifting up their voices in loud complaint. Curt, mildly surprised to find himself in one piece, discovered Keogh kneeling on all fours. He came upright, shaking his head. Two or three other men were dimly visible, but for the moment at least all the fight had been shaken out of them.

"We seem to have arrived," Keogh observed. "At least they stopped the train for us."

Curt strove to match his partner's casualness.

"Maybe those fellows were ticket-takers, and we didn't have any. Now what the—"

Something new was happening, one more unplanned development.

Cattle were suddenly jumping from the car next to the caboose, where they had been confined. They spilled in an increasing stream, having gotten the door all the way open. There had been no chance to close and latch it securely when they climbed to the top.

Taking such leaps in a blind panic could easily have resulted in a long descent and broken bones, but chance favored the frenzied cattle. The car had come to a stop where the surrounding grade sloped up almost to a level with the open door. They were running as they hit, scattering in a mad plunge for freedom.

As though the train were a magnet, a fast-riding crew of men came sweeping up. Pratt's voice boomed angrily above lesser sounds.

Keogh's surprise at this development gave way to understanding. Pratt had lived most of his days in the shadow of the law, and a constant suspicion, the oppression of fear, were not easily cast aside. He'd brought his plan to the threshold of success, which would be climaxed with the loading of the cattle; even in the moment of triumph, it had seemed almost too good to believe.

The chance that something might still go wrong had oppressed him. Riding away with his crew, circling to watch the train begin its long sweep toward the east, rather than head back toward the ranch, Pratt had been in position to lead his crew when the shooting had broken out and the train had halted.

Nor were they the only ones. A rival group, looming at least as large in the night, was converging on the train from another direction. A precisely flat voice boomed out an order in the unemotional twang of a Yankee sergeant, and Keogh's guess was verified. These riders were a detachment from the post. With rumors and reports of trouble and mysterious goings-on rife, Major Yancey Tombright had decided to find out what was going on.

In view of the possibility that there might actually be trouble, he'd given half a hundred of his barracks-weary men the opportunity to ride with him.

The surprise of the two groups meeting was mutual. For Pratt it would have been difficult to imagine a more disheartening or enraging anticlimax to years of planning and work. Despite all the scheming, the meticulous attention to every detail, something had gone wrong. He was faced with failure, and worse.

Save for the untimely intervention of Tombright, his last piece of planning might still have saved the situation, restoring control, sending the train on its way again. But soldiers were a different matter.

His original plan was ruined past retrieving. Pratt was quick to recognize the rival group of riders, to assess the odds and consider his loss. But failure was not yet irrevocable. Confusion was rampant, and the night was a cloak. At least a portion of his vengeance might still be achieved by a counter-move, a literal stampede across the range.

Keogh was too far away to hear the orders which Pratt gave, but he soon understood what they were.

The animals escaping from the one car had given Pratt the idea. Now his crew were riding along the train, pausing to jerk loose the catches and open the car doors.

Not much help was necessary, for the panic-stricken cattle lost no time making a wild rush to escape. Within minutes, bawling, frantic animals were plunging all along the train, some sprawling as they landed, but most regaining their feet to dart away into the night. Some did not survive the jump, but went down under other hurtling bodies, with broken legs or worse.

Yancey Tombright was choking in his wrath, aware that something was going on literally under his nose, but not understanding precisely what it was, although he suspected that once again he was being made a fool of. The confusion, made worse by the plunging cattle, continued long enough for Pratt's purpose. Most of the cars were emptied before a measure of order could be restored.

When it was, Tombright was in command, and most of the other men were under guard, if not under actual arrest. He was all but inarticulate with indignation.

"I intend to find out what the devil is going on," he declared furiously. "There have been far too many shenanigans in this country for too long a time, and I swear somebody's going to sweat for this!" Becoming aware of Keogh, he fixed a frowning glance upon him, while a corporal, retrieving a lantern from one of the train crew, got it alight, a small oasis in the surrounding gloom. "Mr. Keogh, perhaps you'll be able to enlighten me!"

Pratt, along with most of his men, had been rounded up.

"As to what's going on, Major, I guess I'm responsible, and I'll take the full responsibility," he cut in. "When the train stopped, the cars were emptied at my orders. I did not wish to allow them to proceed, to spread plague and destruction across the country, as was intended."

"What's that?" Tombright demanded, bewildered. "What are you saying, sir? Plague? Devil take it, what do you mean?"

"The foot and mouth disease, Major," Pratt returned glibly. Under the circumstances, a show of cooperation would afford him his best chance to win free. Once he was gone in the night, they'd never find him. Otherwise he might be held until the real truth came out.

"I've discovered what's been going on," Pratt continued. "Curt Jackson has a vast, wild scheme for getting vengeance on the country; he seems to hate everyone. Don't ask me why, but it's so. All these cattle have been treated with some sort of a serum, so that within a matter of days they'll develop this disease, sicken and die, spreading infection like a plague among other herds. Hoof and mouth is a disease which, once started, can hardly be controlled. So I worked to stop it from spreading nation-wide, at all costs."

The major was astonished and appalled, only partly understanding what he was being told. He held up a hand and turned again to Keogh.

"What do you know about this, Mr. Keogh? Is there any truth in this wild tale?"

"I'm afraid there is," Keogh admitted. "But it's Pratt here who's at the back of it all; not Jackson, whose ranch and cattle he's stolen. He's the man who wanted vengeance, and it's his scheme. Furthermore, it appears to be fully as bad as he pictures it."

Pratt hesitated, between two minds as to when or how to make a break. If he timed it right, he'd stand a chance, but there could be no further slip-up. Most of his own crew were about, still armed, but even in the uncertain light he could glimpse shock and disbelief on many faces.

They had understood the large-scale rustling, and they hadn't boggled at that. But his plan to spread a plague across the land was beyond anything they'd anticipated. They had assumed that the purpose of inoculating the herd was to guard against disease, not to spread it.

Faced with so appalling a truth, they might not back him in a fight, especially against soldiers. However, he had another trump.

"Mr. Keogh has allowed himself to be badly misinformed. However, on the main point we are in agreement. So if I might venture a suggestion, Major, it would be only an act of prudence to set every available man to rounding up these infected animals without an instant's delay, before they scatter so widely that to control them or the disease becomes impossible."

Tombright's scowl deepened, but he had firmly grasped the salient point.

"You're proving yourself a liar, Mr. Pratt," he said grimly. "First you turn these animals loose to run wild; then you want me to scatter my men to round them up! Sergeant, see to it that neither he nor any of his crew are allowed to escape or to perpetrate further mischief! Is this hoof and mouth disease as bad as he says, Mr. Keogh?"

"I'm afraid so, Major. It is contagious and a bad killer. Even the ground becomes infected, so that the range is unsafe for further use for years afterward."

"Then there's only one thing to do," Tombright decided. "These infected animals must be disposed of as speedily as possible, shot wherever found. Drastic measures are the only means of controlling the thing before it gets out of hand."

21

Another voice, full of dismay, interrupted. Curt Jackson pushed into the light shed by the lantern.

"You can't do that, Major! This scoundrel has stolen my herd, taken over my ranch to work his deviltry, and experimented with the Jackson Herefords as though they were ordinary scrubs! But those cattle are thoroughbreds, sir, blue-ribbon stock, and they belong to me! I'll be worse than ruined if they're butchered indiscriminately!"

Recognizing him, Tombright inclined his head. He still had an imperfect understanding of the plot which had developed almost under his nose, and which had made him a public laughingstock. But he understood enough.

"You may be right, Mr. Jackson, and you have my sympathy. But the public good must come first. Do you agree, Mr. Keogh? The animals, if affected, will die in any case, won't they?"

Keogh nodded. "I'm afraid so."

"Then there is no time to be lost." Tombright

sounded somewhat appalled. "A disagreeable task is never improved by delay or seeking to avoid it. I—"

Again there was an interruption. The Professor pushed forward from the edge of the group.

"You will do better to take it easy, Major. The cattle are all right. There nothing wrong with them is, nor will there be."

Surprisingly, the Professor was sober, and there was a glint half of hate, half of triumph in his eyes as he glanced toward Pratt. The latter, flanked now by a soldier on either side, was staring unbelievingly.

"What's that you're saying?" Pratt shouted. "You're lying! They were all doped last night, as you directed—"

"All were treated, yes," the Professor conceded. "But you are a fool, as I informed you. Do you suppose that you are the only smart one? And you would treat me as a slave, not a co-worker, attributing to me—to me, the one man who ever has worked out the entire progress of the disease, the intelligence of a moron! Deal with me fairly, and I work as squarely in turn. What we dosed them with last night was water, nothing more, nothing less." He waved a negligent hand.

"None will sicken or die. When rounded up again, they still may be shipped and delivered to those who already have paid for them—"

Pratt listened with dismay and disbelief, as the Professor took his revenge. Only as he comprehended the extent of his discomfiture at this man's hands, the totality of his failure, did consternation overtake him. Despite all his careful planning, nothing was working out. Yet the guilt for such a monstrous scheme was already fastened upon him, and that was only a part of the total count. There were the stolen herds, the murdered men—

He broke suddenly from his guards, elbowing one, felling the other with a quick, vicious kick. Others jumped to stop him, and there was a short, vicious melee, in which the train lantern described a wild arc before it shattered on the ground. Then Pratt broke loose, running, dodging, cut off from the horses in the background, the open sweep of plain barred by other men. Desperately he dived for the train itself and dived under a car. Once he was on the far side, the length of the train would temporarily stop pursuit, and with the night for cover, he was confident he could elude them.

One man jerked a gun and fired, but the shot was hasty and wide of the mark. Then, as though on order, the train jerked into motion.

It rolled only a few feet before halting again, uncertainly, but the sudden lurch had been enough. The Professor reached the car, bent down, peering, then straightened, shrugging.

"He will run no further," he observed. "His struggle caused the man with the lantern to swing it, and the engineer up ahead supposed it to be a signal.

This man's luck—how do you say it?—has run out on him."

"You mean I keep this spread—that it's really mine, with no strings attached, and nothing will be held against me for allowing myself to be a pawn of Pratt's?" Hendricks demanded, still disbelieving. "I sure never expected anything like this."

"Well, Pratt turned the ranch over to you, even if he didn't mean it, and now it makes a fair settlement, as everybody seems to agree," Keogh returned. "You'll turn your herd over to Major Tombright at the post, without cost, which seems only fair also, since the Army has already paid for them. That will satisfy him.

"Curt Jackson has his spread back, and most of the money paid for his herd has been recovered, so he's satisfied, too. The buyers get their animals, even if delivery will be somewhat delayed, leaving them no cause for complaint. You've cooperated with us. And in any case, with a wedding coming up in your family, the father of the bride needs a base of operations, as you might say."

Hendricks drew a deep breath, looking to where Curt and Betty walked, forgetful even of the call for supper. The owners of stolen herds had been reimbursed from funds found among Pratt's possessions.

"Having such a ranch will really put me on my feet, and bury a nightmare at the same time," he

said fervently. "And after the way you put a stop
to the biggest steal and most fantastic scheme that
any of us ever dreamed of—well, nobody's disputing
your right to call the tune, Keogh."

"Tut, and two more tuts," Keogh protested depre-
catingly. But Hendricks grinned and went on:

"Those two don't seem much interested in eating.
But I am. And I think there's chicken and dumplings
again. How about it?"

"Lead the way," Keogh agreed. "The way your
wife cooks, there's nothing better than one chicken
leg—unless it's two of them!"